MOOD INDIGO

A Houston Mars Mystery

B.A. Black

To my editor, Stacy, and my writer friends
who kept me sane in 2020.

1.

After the holidays, Houston returns to work. The early January is not as harsh as the late December promised and melts easily into February, clearing the streets slowly of snow. All that's left by the beginning of March—in like a lion—is the early dark of night now closing over the city in 1931.

Chicago breathes steam out into the slowly relenting cold and chugs on like a soldier in the snow, leaving progressively darker slush underfoot as the factories exhale sooty and heated breath.

More homeless bodies crowd the streets as new made success turns into the deepest dark of financial failure. Black Friday, like the black lung that coal miners die from. The internal rot of the boom now burst out.

Houston sees none of it in the passing months. The Winsome money begins to spend itself out as his body heals. He has abandoned his old fascination with the window onto the street; instead losing himself in a new fascination with the past.

He lays it out over his desk in newsprint, finding a half-dozen sources over the four years since he parted company with Lucas Harcourt. His old flame had returned to Houston's life as corpse, the end of the year prior.

Harcourt's body went unclaimed in the municipal morgue until the funeral, kept there by the new detective on the case, Marlowe Ward. He removed it from Detective Exeter after questions arose about his presence as the first officer on scene in a territory that wasn't his. Ex is a known figure in the levy, which raised some uncomfortable questions for him and the Chicago

Police both.

Ward is a by-the-book man. Thorough. But his job was only to determine the cause of death and rule out homicide.

Lucas had more alcohol than blood in his system that night, and the condition of his body at autopsy suggested that it had been the state of affairs for a very long time.

Murder by alcoholism is a nearly impossible endgame and Houston has to admit it's not likely. Too much patience, too imprecise, too much uncertainty when and where it would happen. The autopsy showed some traces of other drug use as well, but the overdose that did him in was plain old illegal alcohol.

In that sense, Houston is convinced it's not a murder. But something reached into Lucas and yanked him down out of the sky, brought him to rest there in that filthy alley. *Something* returned him from the vanished wilds to Chicago, desperate and drinking and alone. Whatever it was, it also kept him away from Houston.

That's what Houston needs to understand. *Why get so close and then stop? Where has Lucas been all these years?*

He finds few clues in his newspaper clippings. In 1928 he turned up in Los Angeles, seeking to move beyond the stage and onto the silver screen. He made it—or so it seems. Houston finds an old billing sheet for a movie with Gary Cooper in it at the top. Lucas is the last name billed, a position like a horse at derby —ready to either surge forward to the lead or fade back to the very last. The title, in artistic and balloony letters, says 'The Honduran', and Houston's never heard of the film. He thinks one of the stylized, illustrated-for-print faces lined up between the lead male and leading lady could be familiar. He stares at it in technicolor, the dot-print showing him only shades of gray.

Since the widespread advent of sound, Hollywood's old guard was out. Charlie Chaplin and Buster Keaton gave way for men and women who had been on Broadway; who already knew how to sound like stars with the audience enrapt.

With some bias, Houston thinks Lucas was made to be a star. On stage, he had a magnetism that pulled you into the fantasy so well you could get utterly lost. Offstage, his eyes pulled you even deeper, wrapping you and him together into a cocoon. Concealing you in a world you couldn't otherwise see.

Very little of what Lucas said was ever true. His past was a confusing jumble of half-truths. When they were involved, Houston collected these all into the handbasket of his thoughts.

Lucas was from Iowa or Indiana. From a small town that had sprung up in the gold rush or begun to die as the war dragged on. He was from a farm in the middle of nowhere, and a need and drive for attention is what compelled him to reach out for stardom with both hands. He was Vaudeville or Shakespearian. Trained or untrained. His family was dead or alive, somewhere far away.

Beyond their meeting in Chicago one wild night at the Sappho after Houston had returned from the war, he can find nothing solid. Between that fixed time and place and the end of Lucas' life in an alley south of the Levy, he has points. An unsolid line dotted across states and dates.

All questions and no answers.

He rearranges the articles on his desk, as if throwing things into a disarray will somehow make them clearer.

"Mars," a voice intrudes, low and careful. "You want a ride home?"

His partner, Salvatore Costanzo, stands in the doorway of his office trailing cigarette smoke and silhouetted in the light from the hall. He's wearing his coat and hat, and Houston realizes it's gotten dark outside. A glance at his old Army watch confirms it's after five.

The offer of a ride home has become a cue—a suggestion be-

3

tween them that they won't spend the night alone. It doesn't happen every day. They're careful. Lately, Houston has seen an increase and he wonders if Sal needs the distraction, or if it's more for Houston's benefit. Either way, they both seem to need it.

It's an unfair amount of stress to put on a new relationship, but it can't last forever anyway. Nothing in this world ever does.

"Mars?" Sal repeats, and Houston realizes he hasn't answered.

"Yeah," he says, not looking forward to the cold ride in Sal's old hay burner. "I'd like that. Thanks, Sal."

Sal watches him with dark, enigmatic eyes as Houston pulls on his coat, carefully negotiating it over his sore shoulder, finally mostly healed and freed from the cast. It's a new coat, purchased at an estate sale, decidedly less torn and shot up than his last one.

Maybe they could talk a little, but Houston's not sure what to say. His words seem often to get lost these days, as his mind tries to wrap around Lucas' death. He was perhaps the only one Houston had left in the world, before Sal. In his mind, a choke point formed around his thoughts when he saw the body in the snow. Now he cannot move past it, captivated and captured behind the barrier.

Houston pulls a half-smoked pack of Chesterfields out of his pocket as he carries his empty cup to the bathroom sink. He lights a cigarette, then rinses the cup clean with the filter balanced between his teeth to pull nicotine into his system. Finally, he sets the mug next to Sal's on the counter, and turns off the hot plate for the coffee.

"I hope we get a case soon," Sal says, breaking the silence as they lock up.

Houston's arm just came out of the cast from the last one. He goes back to the doctor for a check on Friday, two days from now.

"It'd be nice," Houston says. "Even the usual stuff is drying up. You and me are going to have to open a laundry on the side."

Sal follows him down the three flights of stairs to ground level. "You could use a distraction, too. Even starching shirts if that's what it takes."

"I got one," Houston says.

"A distraction from that distraction," Sal grumbles in a lower tone.

Houston's been down this road with Sal in the past; he's not ready to leave it behind yet. There is something *wrong* about it. Something he has to get to the bottom of. He ignores his partner's needling and checks in with Katie Wentz before they go.

"Hey, Miss Wentz," he says, leaning into the telephone switch room.

"Hey, Huey," she says, turning around with a warm expression and her headset on. "Hey, Mr. Costanzo. Funny you guys should come in. I have a guy from the Tribune on your line. I told him I thought you were gone, but he wanted me to ring up to you anyway."

Houston and Sal trade looks. Their phone's been ringing for weeks over the Winsome case. Everybody and their uncle is looking for the inside scoop.

"You want to talk to him?" Miss Wentz asks, one hand on the cord. "He seemed awful earnest."

"Take a message, please," Sal says politely. "We're out for the evening. Thanks, Katie."

Sal flashes her a smile that belongs in the movies, and Houston's heart skips a little beat even as a bystander. He's sure that's how Sal always gets his way.

"Okay, Mr. Costanzo," Miss Wentz says, twinkling her eager

smile back at him. "Have a good night. You too, Huey."

Houston tries not to grimace at the nickname. "Goodnight, Miss Wentz."

Sal steps out into the street ahead of Houston, leading the way to his car parked at the curb in front of the building. Far from the pre-holiday bustle, downtown Chicago has settled back into the hibernal pattern of its winters, just beginning to wake for spring. The nights are early dark and heavy. From somewhere, Houston can hear blues—the sad, slow rise and swell of trumpet and saxophone, the new depression pulse of the city.

The car door hinges shriek open stiffly in the cold, discordant. The black leather seat is freezing, even through the layers of Houston's clothes and coat. He pulls the door shut again, ringing the impact through the whole frame of the car.

Sal looks at him for a long moment, eyes dark and deep. Something stays unsaid, and Sal starts the car.

They pull up outside Sal's building, parking in the lot. Houston's thoughts feel sluggish and heavy, only dimly focused. He's still working on the problem in a less intent way. Churning it over like a cook stirring ingredients into a batter.

"Hobbes," Sal says, and his voice pulls Houston up from the blank-yet-busy part of his mind. Houston looks over, starting to reach for the lever to open the door.

Sal is looking directly at him, watching him with sharp attention. He hasn't made any effort to get out of the car—instead he leans toward Houston, reaching over and getting his hands tangled up in the front lapels of Houston's coat and pulling him across the seat into his arms. He doesn't—or can't—say anything. Instead he just holds Houston tightly for a long time.

"Sal, I'm okay," Houston says, with his face pressed into Sal's neck and the surprising relief of Sal's cologne washing over him. It's something pine-and-dusk scented, expensively faint.

"Sometimes, I wonder," Sal says, so low it's only their proximity that makes it clear.

For a moment, it's easy and warm—comforting, even. A chance for Houston to let his muscles relax out of the tension he's held them in since the Winsome case.

Then, it's stifling. Houston pulls back. "Getting cold out here."

"Sure," Sal says.

They both unfossilize, returning to action like two of Medusa's men released at last from their prisons of statuary. The doors clunk open, then ring closed with a sharp sound in the cold air.

"How's it feel to have that cast off your arm?" Sal says, striking up a conversation with Houston for the sake of appearances as they enter his apartment building. If they look animated enough, they can avoid conversation with the doorman. Better not to connect, to avoid the feelings of guilt. To avoid being seen too often together in the evenings *before* and the mornings *after*.

"Lighter," Houston says. It still aches if he uses it too much, and in the cold. It was off at last, however. It seemed interminable while he was wearing it. "Doc says I'll need physical therapy to get it back to strength."

"Gonna hit the gym, finally?" Sal asks. The doorman tips his hat and admits them without any comments that might interrupt their meaningless conversation.

"I called it quits with the gym after boot camp," Houston says.

Sal laughs at him, but his hand goes to the small of his own back in an absent, telling gesture.

"What'd you do about it?" Houston asks him as they wait for the elevator.

"I went to the gym," Sal says, cracking wise. "Used to work until the pain made me want to scream."

He says it with a light tone, but Houston senses honesty in the statement.

"I got that Swedish massage a lot too," Sal continues, still with humor. "Guess I was just out for pain."

"Don't I know that," Houston mutters. "You still are, most days."

The elevator appears behind the gate, and the bellboy stops it with a soft chime, swinging open the gate to let out two ladies in last years fashion before Houston and Sal step in.

"Home, please," Sal tells the kid.

"You got it, Mr. Costanzo," the boy says. He glances around the faded art-deco lobby for signs of any other potential passengers before he closes the gate and works the lever, causing the elevator to rise.

"Massage, huh?" Houston continues the conversation as they ascend. "Did it work?"

"Hurt like hell," Sal says. "But they say what doesn't kill you...."

Houston will think about it. It may well not matter. His arm was only casted up for a couple of months. His shoulder will be stiff for a while, that's all.

At the right floor, the bellboy stops the elevator and Sal tips him a couple pennies before they both get off.

In the hall, he leans over to murmur in Houston's ear. "The massages weren't *all* bad, you know."

Houston chuckles. "It's a little different to get a shoulder rub, pal."

"I got a girl who knows a guy shouldn't be stopped up too long, for his health," Sal says, admitting them into his apartment. The space is a familiar, half-finished array of projects. "I'd ask if you

MOOD INDIGO

wanted her number, but I know better."

Houston glances over at the partially painted wall and its attending mess of drop cloth and solidified paint-can-and-brush. It's like part of an avant-gard painting itself: *Still Life With Mess*.

"You want a beer?" Sal calls, moving deeper into his apartment, toward the ice-box he struggles to finance the ice for every few days. The water itself is cheap—cut from the usually frozen shoreline of the Lake crawling up alongside the belly of the city. The cost is for purity and labor—the tireless work of the ice man lugging blocks up the unending city floors with dollies and tongs.

"Do you have any?" Houston asks, surprised.

"Sure, but don't ask how old it is."

"How old *is* it?" Houston replies on cue.

"It's a previous vintage," Sal says, poking his head into the ice-box, producing two dark brown bottles without labels or dates. "But enjoyable, despite the dust."

Houston accepts the gift, trying to settle his spinning mind here in the moment. Sal's uncharacteristic gesture of care surprises him. Houston knows he's been distant, but he didn't think it was worth any concern, especially to Sal, who seems content to avoid any sign of involvement beyond the most private. It was maybe one of the best qualities of Sal's personality, aside from his quiet mystery and his intuition for discretion.

Sal passes him a churchkey and they pry the tops off their beers as Houston stumbles over what to say, starting a half-dozen conversations in his thoughts and finding none of them to be adequate.

He takes a long pull from the neck of the bottle instead, excusing himself against the tide of bitter and bubbles and finding that Sal's as good as his word. The beer is fine. They stand in Sal's kitchen, dirty with dishes and the stains of the glorious past, and circle each other like the rims of their bottles, quiet and companionable as two men who know each other so intimately can be in such tense and spidery air.

"How's Chop Suey?" Sal tries.

This is safe territory.

"He hasn't tried to go out once since the cold snap half-froze him," Houston says. "After losing the tips of both his ears, can't say I blame him."

"Well, he's got it good with you," Sal says. "You're soft."

They're circling again now. Electrifying each other like the air currents of a spring thunderstorm. Sal leads the conversation out of the kitchen up the short hallway and into unseen territory, into his windowless bedroom. It's a risk every time, but Houston's learned to relax into this; they have excuses of friendship and partnership. The rest is caution.

When the door is closed behind them, Sal takes Houston's beer and seals the taste between their mouths and caution goes to the side, set on Sal's tie-strewn and well-ringed dresser top next to the ashtray.

Where it belongs.

In the darkness and aftermath, Houston catches his breath and looks up at the constellation of stains on Sal's ceiling. He can hear Sal sighing and chugging to a stop like an overworked locomotive as he reels his focus back in.

The air is sticky and heavy with sex, the aftersmell like the ocean shore—salt and brine and your own sweat melting the cologne off your body. The old memories are nearly as sticky-heavy in his mind as the humidity was on Houston's breath—a pressure on his chest.

How often, and in how many places did Houston lay like this when Lucas was the guiding light over the shore of his life? Smooth sailing over-by-inches the treacherous rocks beneath the surface of reality. The risks seemed small, then, and easy. There was always another party, always the Sappho or the Selene, always the implicit understanding that as long as times were that good, everyone was too deep in their own sand castles to look up and sound an alarm.

Prohibition and the Depression worked like a one-two punch. The fun faded; the distractions vanished and eyes came open. Misery sought to make others miserable.

By the time all of it came crashing down, Lucas was already gone. He'd gone before the tide, but it caught him anyway and smashed his frozen body right back against the shore from which he'd departed.

Odysseus had come home.

Sal reaches for Houston before the tight feeling in his chest can drown him, curling his body against Houston with a quiet, satisfied sound that makes Houston feel like a shipwreck in time and space, disconnected by all but one frail string.

2.

The message is waiting on the floor of his office the next day when Houston arrives. It—and several others—wait in a stack tied in a twine bow. Miss Wentz doesn't believe in the rubber band, claiming it lacks the personal touch that she prides herself on.

Houston claims the bundle—a daily delivery that outstrips some of their previous *weeks*, and takes it to his desk for a pass through to check for any cases.

"Any luck?" Sal asks, standing in the hall between offices and shrugging his coat off his lean, powerful shoulders. It's a cat's motion, a captivating one for Houston.

"Lots of reporters," Houston says.

"Well, the Winsome hearing," Sal says, as if it's the answer to everything.

"Sure, but it doesn't pay the bills."

"Might pay something." Sal leans in Houston's office doorway, one shoulder pressed to the frame. "You going to talk to any of them?"

Houston holds up the stack. "Mars—very interested in your take on the Charles Winsome affair. Contact me at the Tribune. -D. O'Halloran."

"Doesn't say anything about money," Sal says. "*Tribune*'s gone crooked since the collapse anyway."

"Sal, none of 'em say anything about money. Nobody's got any. Besides, I wouldn't do it anyway."

Sal grins at him, a slow, curving thing. It reminds Houston of what he looks like at the height of pleasure. "Too close to home?"

"Dirt over stone over dirt," Houston agrees. "Only the stone's so thin a shovel would break through. You're the one who told me not to piss in my own garden."

"Mmm-hmm," Sal agrees.

A few minutes later, Houston gets up to turn on the boiler plate under the percolator, sending new water back through yesterday's grounds. The resulting coffee is stale and unsatisfying, but until they get another case, they'll have to make things stretch.

They've gotten good at it.

Houston spreads the newspaper articles over his desk again, wincing at the lingering stiffness in his shoulder. He considers them as a group. The most recent is an interview about two years ago, a short piece about the locals from Chicago getting into the movie industry. Houston reads it for the dozenth time.

Local stars 'in' at the movies this year!

Hollywood fans might see a few familiar faces on the big screen this year if they pay attention. Several former Majestic stars have made their way west to Hollywood and broken into the big time, starring alongside Hollywood greats like Gary Cooper and Jean Gabin...

It's a fluff piece, a catalog of boasts about the Chicago-raised talent that had made it *somewhere*, carefully ignoring the dozens that saw big praise in the papers and yet now are passed over by even the *Tribune*. None of their rising star predictions have come through.

"'I just went for it," local Lucas Harcourt told the Tribune in a private interview. "I thought 'what's the use of sitting around Chicago's Broadway? We all know where the future is.'"

The actor went on to confide, "It's tough out there, but there's real opportunity. You just have to shake the right hands, make the right moves. And, of course, have some talent."

The words hardly sound like Lucas to Houston, he can't quite summon the old ghost of his voice anymore. Houston takes a deep breath, and for a moment, he wonders what he's doing. Staring at articles in his cold office, listening to the jazz come out-of-place and cheerful from Sal's office across the hall, spinning away on his Victrola.

I'm crazy, Houston thinks. *He just didn't make it, that's all. Flew too close to the sun and melted all the wax.*

He's about to sweep all the articles together and into his drawer, to mark the whole ordeal finally done when something catches his eye about that article on top. The reporter's byline under the headline and date—D. O'Halloran.

Houston stares at the name for a moment, transfixed by an idea like a bug on a pin. He tries to resist it, tries to tell himself it's only a coincidence, these things happen all the time. Of course he was bound to come across a familiar name, he was looking at newspaper articles after all. But the sensation of need stabs right through his middle, piercing neatly beneath his sternum to pin the idea against his ribcage.

He puts the articles away, and reaches down into the void of his trash basket, fishing out the crumpled up paper with Miss Wentz's handwriting on it, and smooths it back out on his desk.

After agonizing for a week, Houston agrees to meet the reporter at the counter of an old bar at the levy. He's spent the time reviewing the cost and depth of the sale of his morals, turning the simple decision into a protracted one. Up the street, he can see the Lee-Lee's sign. Now the building is crouched over the street, mouth open and screened in, waiting for someone to step inside and wake the smoking monster that waits in the basement.

Houston is glad he's come alone. Sal has washed his hands of this crusade, but Houston has to come. He has to *know*. It's the latest article about Lucas, the freshest trail before his body was found three months and three blocks ago.

The street is covered in snow as it was then, the result of a huge storm on the seventh, Houston closes his eyes and remembers the body under a sheet. Detective Exeter asked him why there was a picture of him in the pocket of a dead man's suit. Houston is still struggling to answer that, all these months later.

Ex said, Houston remembers the words now as he pulls an old, half-smoked Chesterfield out of his checkbook pocket, *bad luck and bad timing follow you, Detective Mars.*

It doesn't matter.

"Hey, Mac," a voice says, pulling Houston out of his thoughts. The proprietor in a paper hat and a greasy mustache. "What are you having?"

"Beer?" Houston asks, hoping.

"Sody-pop," the soda jerk says, indicating a row of taps now with brightly colored logos on the handles. Pepsi, Coca-Cola, Moxie. "It's good for the health."

Houston's only sure it builds constitution by pugilism, but he orders a tall, bitter glass of Moxie—"The orange one"—so he doesn't get kicked out.

The reporter is late. A not-mousy man making an attempt to look smart in tortoise-rimmed specs and a half-beat hat. He has a pencil—half gnawed and eraserless—jammed into the band where most wear press passes. The pass itself is nowhere to be seen. Probably, south of the Levy, service and solicitations got spotty if you paraded as a reporter. Better stories if you were just Joe or Mac. He spots Houston and seems to recognize him.

"Detective Mars," he says, offering his hand. "I'm Dan O'Halloran from the *Tribune*. Thanks for meeting me."

Houston takes his offered grip. The handshake is neither aggressive nor weak, but calculatedly average.

Dan O'Halloran wears his middle age like it's a much older coat. Houston would guess he's in his thirties, but he cultures an experienced air. Houston wonders if that's a defense mechanism— a way to be the youngest surviving reporter in any room these days. Cutbacks have left everyone younger on the street—tenure has only protected the ancients. As a result, the papers are all full of bland and safe news, returning to a style that was popular before the turn of the century. They refuse to report on anything more interesting than all the misery of the depression and foreign affairs.

Houston wonders how O'Halloran remains protected. Wonders if it's a sordid story or a triumphant one.

If he gets an answer he likes to his first questions, he'll ask, but he'll do it after he knows about Lucas.

"Why's this interesting to you?" Houston asks as O'Halloran swings himself up onto the stool just around the corner from him. "Every reporter in the city is covering the Winsome case."

"But not every reporter has your statement on the issue, Detective Mars. I know for a fact that I'm the only one you ever called back—and with the results of the hearing leading to a real trial, the time is right to revisit the facts. So, lucky break that I have something you need, huh?"

"Lucky," Houston agrees, trying to get a better measure of the man sitting across from him. O'Halloran orders a Pepsi. Both of them are probably wishing for a little more than soda.

O'Halloran's expression is hard to read. His eyes are intensely green, but his eyelids seem almost perpetually heavy. It softens the keen features from predatory to shy. Houston's seen the same look on foxes when he was a kid. After they killed all the chickens in the coop and laid down in the yard to gnaw the bones even while his father got the gun. They'd watched with that *what-are-you-gonna-do-about-it* expression until they were absolutely satisfied before running. About half the time, they still got away. Something in the nature of foxes meant you didn't win, even if the blast from the shotgun scattered them into blood and insides, discorporated like one of those future movies at the nickel show.

"Detective Mars?" O'Halloran prods, producing a beat up reporter's pad, and pulling the chewed up pencil out of his hatband. "You still with me?"

"Sorry," Houston says, wetting his mouth with bitter cola, swallowing it. "I'm ready for your questions."

"Why were you at the Sappho before the body was discovered, Mr. Mars?"

It takes Houston a moment to figure out *which* body O'Halloran means—of course he's talking about Charles Winsome. That's the case Houston agreed to discuss with him. But his mind brings up an image of that dark alley a few blocks away, of pulling the sheet back to reveal features almost too changed to recognize...

Dan O'Halloran is watching him with piercing, attentive green eyes lancing out from beneath the brim of his hat, taking in Houston's every breath, all his expressions.

"Jeez, O'Halloran," Houston says. "You know why I was there. You can't *print* that—the man's dead, but his wife ain't."

"So you were looking for Charles Winsome," O'Halloran confirms. He doesn't mark it on his pad, but he doesn't put down his pencil either.

"Yes," Houston resists the urge to ask *"what else would I be doing there?"* He recognizes it as a trap of words, the same kind he might lay with a suspect in interview.

"You had reason to believe he might be there?" O'Halloran presses.

17

"We questioned a friend of his. Eddie—one of the other victims of the Winsome brothers," Houston says. He tears his gaze away from O'Halloran's intent expression and tries to banish that image from his mind—Eddie laid out in his silk underwear and robe, mangled in his chair like a sacrifice left on a throne.

Houston takes a sip of the harsh, medicinal tasting Moxie to wash the sour taste out of his mouth. "He pointed us to the Sappho and Levytown. I believe that was just a ploy to send us the other direction."

"That so?" O'Halloran is back to writing now, his pencil moving over the slim page of his notepad. "So he wasn't a homosexual?"

"He didn't frequent the Sappho," Houston evades.

Another mark on the paper. O'Halloran says, "You checked a few other places of that ilk on the same day, right before Charles turned up dead in that neighborhood."

"Nobody down there knew him."

"Folks tend to be pretty secretive in those establishments. You're sure about the information you got?"

"I'm sure."

"*How* are you sure?" O'Halloran presses, glancing up from his pad.

Houston suddenly realizes it's all a game. O'Halloran already knows *something*. "What are you driving at?"

"What if I told you I know *you* frequented the Sappho in the past?"

"That so?" Houston keeps his voice level as possible.

O'Halloran watches him sharply, apparently waiting for his reaction. What he gets doesn't seem to discourage him. He lowers his tone and continues, "You used to frequent the place with that actor you're so keen to grill me about."

Houston doesn't know what to say. He can hardly deny it. "Where'd you hear that?"

O'Halloran makes a note on his pad—something short. He looks up slowly, using the brim of his hat to best effect. It reveals his green eyes slowly. "You can deny it, I just find it strange—like you would—some guy you used to frequent the place with turns up dead a block away, and you're the first on the scene."

"What are you implying?" Houston asks. The cause of death was exposure, and he has an alibi—a couple of them—for that evening.

"I'm not implying," O'Halloran says. He leans on the counter, putting his elbow up next to his empty soda glass. "I'm *asking*. Do you want to go someplace less public and talk about the connection?"

Houston tries to read that sleepy gaze, tries to understand what the motivation behind O'Halloran is here—blackmail? Does he want to try and spin Lucas' death into a murder?

"You said you wanted to talk about the Winsome case," Houston says.

"Sure," O'Halloran says. "And you said you wanted to talk about Lucas Harcourt. We're talking about him. It's not my fault I'm well informed on the subject."

"Did Lucas tell you..." Houston says, suddenly struck—it feels like a betrayal. Did Lucas speak about Houston to others? Did he sell their secrets, tell people about their relationship?

Dan O'Halloran gets up, pulling his wallet out of his coat. He looks at the soda jerk then gives Houston a piercing glance—one that tells him to shut up. To *stop talking* before he says something he regrets in public.

"Let's continue this discussion in private," O'Halloran says. He pays for his soda and leaves a small tip—maybe if he's a black-mailer, it explains how he can afford to. How he's still in business with a paper full of reporters 20 years his senior.

Houston pays too, distracted, and follows him out.

O'Halloran lives in an honest-to-goodness house in the suburbs —nothing to write home about. It's one of those kit houses from an earlier decade—an economical solution to the thousands of new families that found themselves formed after the triumphant return of the soldiers from war. A place to house the expected population boom.

It's a simple floor plan, one of those homes that runs front to back in an easily navigated line. The front door comes off an elevated deck into a small vestibule for coats and hats and then into the living room. The house is well kept-up, despite the hard times, but Houston notices that the interior is sparsely inhabited by furniture. Familiarity with the stock floor plan tells Houston it's a two bedroom joint, but he sees no sign of other occupants.

Houston scrapes off his boots on the mat and tries to form a real picture of O'Halloran from the interior of his home. *A bachelor*, he decides, *and a neat and practical one.*

"When you interviewed Lucas..." Houston begins the sentence without being certain of exactly how it's going to end, his gaze sweeping over the pleasant—feminine—wallpaper that covers the living room wall. O'Halloran stands just inside the doorway, folding his coat up and dropping it into the bottom of the closet rather than putting it onto one of the four hangers that occupy the rod inside it. "Was he here, in Chicago?"

It seems to take O'Halloran a moment to shift gears from wherever his thoughts were to the answer to this question. "What do you mean?"

"I mean, did you speak to him in person for that newspaper piece or did you talk to him on the phone, two years ago?" Houston clarifies.

O'Halloran steps back around Houston in the entryway and closes the door behind him. Houston doesn't take off his coat, doesn't move from the entryway, even as the reporter moves deeper into the living room. He feels hesitant to be here, wary of the whole situation.

"He was here, Detective Mars," O'Halloran says. "But he was flighty about it. He said he couldn't stay long, that he had to be careful where he went in the city. I got the impression he was avoiding someone. At the time, I thought maybe he owed somebody in the Mob money, or maybe he knew a cop in the wrong way, if you know what I mean."

Houston isn't sure that he does. There's something off about O'Halloran, something off about this whole situation that Houston can't quite put his finger on.

"Come on a little deeper inside," O'Halloran invites. "Listen, Detective, it's not the Ritz-Carlton, but it's not a cave. I think you have the wrong idea."

"What's the right idea?" Houston asks, but he dares a step farther, off of the sturdy tile and onto the soft, deep rug in the living room.

In contrast with the flowery wallpaper, there's a couch and a pair of easy chairs in tartan plaid arranged companionably around a low table with coffee cup rings engraved on the venerable surface. Houston gets the feeling that O'Halloran works here, though he may have an office elsewhere. The setup—couch facing chairs, and no sign of a radio or other distractions—is specifically for interviews.

"Lucas was trying to keep away from *you*, wasn't he?" O'Halloran asks, instead of answering Houston's question. "It wasn't that he was in trouble, it was that he didn't want you to see him."

Houston bristles at the idea, feeling the hair on the back of his neck stand up like an angry dog's and his fists get tight at his sides. It must show on his face, because O'Halloran reacts.

"Ease up," O'Halloran says, displaying his ink-stained hands palm-out in a peacemaking gesture. "Sit down and listen to me before you get so defensive. He didn't want you to see him be-cause he didn't want you to see what had happened to him."

"What had happened-?" Houston starts—it pulls him out of his well-deep anger. Throws a rope down for his sensibility to get up out of his own stubborn hard-headedness.

"Sit down, Detective," O'Halloran says in a softer tone. "I'll tell you the whole story."

Despite his misgivings, and the faint alarm bells ringing some-where in the back of his brain, warning Houston like an air-raid siren that it's better if he doesn't know, Houston relents. *I could still walk away from this. Pull myself out of involvement with the whole case if I just refuse to listen. This is nothing—a desperate at-tempt to fish for information.* Houston pulls his coat off, folding it over his arm like a shield, and sits down on the couch.

O'Halloran takes his hat off before he occupies one of the easy chairs, sitting down comfortably and heavily, like it's a load of weight off his shoulders, as if he's had a long satisfying day. Houston checks his watch, and finds it's only just past two in the afternoon.

Without the hat, Dan O'Halloran looks a little softer, a little more earnest. He leans forward, feet apart and elbows on his knees with his hands pressed together to hang between his shins as he considers Houston, stepping out onto uncertain ground.

"I spoke to Lucas here," he says. "One of his friends pointed me out to him, oh, say, about three days before my article was due."

He sounds evasive, careful. Like he's checking the depth of something before he jumps in. Houston finally changes track in his mind—what is the mystery of Dan O'Halloran, rather than what he held about Lucas and Houston's own past.

"He said what I put in the article, on-record," O'Halloran continues, "but he said some other things, too. Broke my heart a little. He said that he did some pretty despicable things to get what he wanted in Hollywood. That some pretty despicable things were done *to* him. Nothing I like to repeat."

Suddenly, Houston realizes with perfect clarity what O'Halloran's dancing around. All that driving earlier—his pointed line of inquiry. Houston could laugh, or scream, or walk out the door right now.

"You slept with him," Houston says.

O'Halloran smiles; it's not a warm smile, but there's a little triumph in it.

"You did too," he returns the accusation. "Just not for a story."

Houston sits back against the couch and tries to re-route his thoughts. There should be anger, jealousy, outrage maybe—but he'd known Lucas. Known all the ways his heart would fly away from Houston in the past. At the point they're talking about, Houston was working hard and looking down; Lucas was long gone. All he can summon up is a sterile acceptance of the notion, and a vague curiosity at what Dan's time with Lucas revealed.

With a sick twist forming in his belly, he realizes that he wants what Lucas left—not just the information that O'Halloran is offering, but the rest he is suggesting implicitly by taking Houston into his confidence about the exact nature of the exchange between him and Lucas. He takes a deep breath, trying to even his own keel. "Alright. Are you going to put any of this in your paper?"

O'Halloran gives him a winning grin, and all the fox is back in him now. "You think it'd sell papers?"

"Not so fast as if I told your senior reporters that you propositioned me in your own home."

"Say," O'Halloran says. "Did I do that? What an idea."

There's a moment of hesitation between them where each accepts the idea that their fencing has placed in each other's minds, the way such casual encounters have played out a hundred times for Houston in the past. Each still trying to push down the nerves, trying to let the rest of the emotions bloom over the well-instilled fear, over the reserve society has instilled on men like them.

"So I propositioned you," O'Halloran continues. "How'd it play out?"

They both know the answer, Houston thinks, but he strings the line out a little further. Now it's all the easy sensation of reeling in a well-hooked fish; you had to fight a little, on both ends. There's always a struggle that pleasurably taxes the muscles, that pulls until you forget to think about anything else.

"Depends on what you've got to drink," Houston says, reaching up to loosen his tie.

Later, closer. With the well-soaked taste of whiskey against Houston's tongue and the pleasure of the knowledge that he's enjoyed a far better vintage than he would have in any underground speakeasy, Houston feels placated. His blood's warm, his body alert and excited by O'Halloran's proximity.

The fight's past, anyway, and O'Halloran pushes Mars in backsteps like a bad waltz through the narrow hallway and into his bedroom, which lacks any sign of the softer touches in the living room. Houston hits the bed-rail with the backs of his thighs, and O'Halloran laughs against his mouth, pushing him over with surprising strength.

They're about equal height, Houston is surprised to find—O'Halloran affects a harmlessness, holds himself in a way that suggests he isn't a threat while his eyes do all the menacing. Up close, Houston can see there's flecks of dark in the green.

He turns his head when O'Halloran tries to close their lips together—that intimacy feels wrong, and the ghost of O'Halloran's whiskey-softened breath over Houston's neck is enough to almost remind him of his commitments.

Then O'Halloran gets his hand on the fly of Houston's suit trousers, grabbing firmly for the erection clothed there and squeezing enough to get through the half-drunk haze, to leave Houston groaning and pulling at O'Halloran's undershirt, trying to turn the tide.

"*There* you are," O'Halloran says. "Jeez."

Houston arches up, and pulls until they both have to disengage in order to get their clothes off, trying to keep his thoughts in the here and now.

"He talked about you, you know," O'Halloran tantalizes. Houston looks up to see him with his hair in a disarray, standing back from the bed with his hands on his own trouser-button and twisting his hips out of his pants and boxers.

O'Halloran has an arrow-straight body, trim despite a job that usually lends a certain softness in the middle. He's not unattractive, with a thatch of brassy chest hair that draws a line down his belly to the darker nest of curls over his hard cock. It reaches upward on a faint curve, a promising jut that makes Houston want to curl his hand around it, to weigh it against his palm and see if it has more yet to grow.

O'Halloran catches him looking, giving Houston a satisfied grin that could peel paint. Houston looks away, trying to quell the irritation that heats his blood up in a way he's not used to. It's the wrong sort of excitement—more like Houston's about to get into a fight, like the feeling he got once when he was looking out over the stretch of no-man's-land he had to cross and hoping there were no snipers—or one really good one.

He pulls his own pants off but leaves his shirt on, one last barrier against real intimacy—that isn't what this is about—and reaches for O'Halloran as the reporter joins him on the bed. There's an old-cologne smell in the sheets, clean and starch, and that strikes Houston most of all.

O'Halloran behaves as if he's the sort of person who finds himself entangled every week with a different subject, but Houston sees all the signs of false bravado. When they're too close for Houston to see him properly, with Houston's knee tangled between O'Halloran's own, shifting at the feeling of nimble and unfamiliar fingers exploring his back. They play a hot, electric thrill down his spine, running hot and cold until he feels his body respond. The sensation, like danger and heat and all wrapped up, wakes something primal in him. Houston presses his mouth against the hot skin over O'Halloran's collarbone and bites down, quick, hard.

O'Halloran pulls breath, breathes it out, entreats softly as his hand goes down between them and spider-crawls his fingers low on Houston's stomach. "Houston."

It's wrong, but his heated palm against the head of Houston's cock smooths over the shock of his own name—though not the one he's used to hearing in intimacy.

"O'Halloran, shit," Houston tries to warn him off.

"You can call me Dan."

Houston doesn't call him anything, instead rocking his hips up, forward, presses his length into O'Halloran's grip. He just chases his pleasure, pushes his body against it until O'Halloran presses him over onto his back, reaching for something in the nightstand.

"What'd he tell you?" Houston asks, as his mind unmoors from a sensible bearing, as O'Halloran swings his narrow hips over Houston's waist and rocks his body once side to side as if measuring Houston's span.

O'Halloran looks down the length of his chest, looks straight into Houston as if he were still fully clothed and not tracing the underside of his cock over Houston's stomach in a slow slide back and forth as he works something slick and sticky between his hands to warm it up. There's no surprise, no disgust in his gaze even as Houston refuses to take the question back. He seems almost to have expected it, as he reaches back to close his hand over Houston's cock to spread the slick over it.

"He said he didn't want you to see what he'd become," O'Halloran tells him, softly.

In the aftermath, with his back pressed against the reporter's warm front and a film of hot-but-cooling sweat between them, Houston chases ghosts. His thoughts, which by all rights should be satisfied and turning towards sleep revolve on the point of what Lucas must have found here. Did he come to find satisfaction like this? Was it more tantalizing agony?

Houston, laying where Lucas must have lain, having some version of what Lucas had—which Houston deeply desires in a dark compulsion to follow the steps Lucas made before he truly disappeared—stirs his restless thoughts. Did he stretch his hand over the white—risky color for a man of O'Halloran's bent—bedspread and feel like he was once again in control of his own life?

Houston closes his eyes until the sluggish wistfulness passes. O'Halloran's breath is an even rhythm that soothes Houston in spite of his racing mind. One of them, anyway, has reached satisfaction. Houston hopes Lucas did.

After a time, he gets up, turning into the small kit-house master bathroom. There's still afternoon light coming in the small frosted window, but it's pale and hazy. The dim of evening is upon them.

Houston scrubs the oily residue of lubricant from his body with a washcloth, persisting until all traces are neatly contained on one well-fouled scrap of terrycloth, which he throws impolitely into the shower stall with a wet sound before returning to bed.

O'Halloran's sitting up now, his lazy gaze flicking toward Houston as he returns. He's smoking a cigarette and filling the room with the burnt paper smell of a fresh light.

It's Lucas' brand.

"Tell me the rest," Houston says, sitting his half-naked body down on the bed next to O'Halloran's. In the late light that pushes through the thin curtains, the almost-red of O'Halloran's brassy brown hair shows.

"You sure you really want to know?" O'Halloran asks him. "I have a little, but it's pretty rough."

Houston picks up O'Halloran's pack of cigarettes from the rumpled bedspread and O'Halloran sets his cut-glass ashtray in the valley that forms between their naked bodies.

"Yeah," Houston leans back against the headboard in a parody of companionable aftermath. "Tell me the whole story."

O'Halloran takes a moment, seeming to line everything up in his head, breathing his small cloud of smoke as he thinks things over. "He said Los Angeles was different than what he expected, that everything's built on favors. Once someone gets a position of power up there, they'll make you dance for every little thing you want."

The sleepy, heavy-lidded look is back on O'Halloran's features now, thoughtful and sedate. Houston can see past it now, still see the sharp mind working and churning away, trying to find a connection wherever he can, to ferret out the story like it was some kind of nuisance animal or a pestilence.

"I asked him if he meant more than just a little slaving and begging," O'Halloran says. "I know a little bit about sucking cock to get where you need to be. I had a feeling I wasn't gonna like the answer."

Here's the answer to Houston's earlier question of how a man O'Halloran's age still had his job, though he's not sure it's wholly literal. O'Halloran's gaze is a mile away, still churning through his own memories for insight into Lucas.

"It was more than that," O'Halloran says, and there's genuine sympathy in his tone. "The kid—hell, *kid.* You know how old he was. He looked haunted, injured in a way. Whatever it *was* out there in L.A., it was bad."

Houston's insides twist around in a sickening motion. "Why'd he go back? If he got out to make it here for an interview, he could have—"

"Could have nothing," O'Halloran says. "He went back the same reason I do every day—what he wanted was the carrot, what he had to do to get there was the damn stick. After a while of that, you stop caring how hard it lands on your body. All you can see is that damned carrot. He *had* to go back."

Houston's not sure if they're talking about Lucas anymore. He lets the silence stretch on for a moment, waiting to see what else O'Halloran will give him. He pulls the familiar taste of smoke over his tongue, thinking back to moments like this that he shared in the past, the spaces between flights of fancy where Lucas would settle down to rest.

"Who was it?" Houston asks, when O'Halloran doesn't volunteer anything.

"Producer, I think. He was cagey about it—gets that way sometimes when someone knows you're a reporter." O'Halloran slides a pointed look in Houston's direction. "Anyway, he was here and gone, and he hardly stopped moving the whole time. I tried to check up on him a couple of months later, but he wouldn't answer my calls."

He pauses a beat, then adds, "And I didn't even paint an unflattering picture of him in print."

"Do you know where he was living?" Houston asks, feeling a surge of hope—maybe some new trail was about to open up out of all of this. Maybe a way to make it back, find out who turned Lucas over so cruelly that he forgot his wings and starved in the cage.

O'Halloran looks thoughtful. "Yeah, I have an address. I told him he should leave one in case any interest turned up from the article, or I had any followup questions. He said something about a room-mate too."

Houston waits expectantly, letting the weight of his gaze do the work his words can't.

Stubbing the cigarette out in the ashtray, O'Halloran at last makes a move to get up from the bed. "Look, despite all this, and I know it's hardly my business, but he's dead, Detective. It wasn't murder, it's just the world these days. If you're fragile—"

"Someone *made* him fragile," Houston says, hearing the sharp sound of his own voice like a surprise. He gets up too, stuffing the filter end of the burning cigarette into his mouth and reaching for his pants. Suddenly, the lassitude in his body has begun to turn toxic and poison, the inactivity of post-intercourse haze burns him. "Someone *did* this to him, O'Halloran, and I want to know who."

"Jeez," O'Halloran says, and that's it. It encompasses a lot— enough that Houston gets the wind of all he means. Of all he's just revealed of his own weakness in front of a predator. O'Halloran looks up from rifling the drawer of his bedside table, producing a thick handful of reporter's notebooks held together with a few rubber bands. His expression says he knows what drives Houston's determination, and it's the sort of information you didn't want someone with ties to the *Tribune* to know.

Houston buttons his pants and reaches for his socks while O'Halloran flips through one of the notebooks with dates on the front roughly corresponding to the timeframe of the article in question. It's more organized than Houston would have guessed, given the way the notes in his thin, pointed hand dash themselves at odd angles over the pages, written in the reporter's own mix of shorthand and exact quotes.

"Here," O'Halloran says, finding the right page. He lays the pad on top of the night stand, digs a pencil out of his drawer, and copies the address onto a blank page for Houston before tearing it out, folding it once and passing it over.

Houston tucks it into his shirt pocket, against his heart.

"So, Charles Winsome, you said he didn't go to the Sappho, and I know you're right," O'Halloran presses, sitting back down on the edge of the bed. His current notebook and pencil are balanced casually over his bare thigh. "But he was a *company man* anyway, right?"

"Christ," Houston says. "You can't print that."

O'Halloran smiles a little, slyly. "No one else is printing it, it'd be a break if *I* did."

"What about Alfreda Winsome?" Houston says, picking up his tie from the floor. "If you put that in the papers, what'll it do to her?"

"She won't answer my calls," O'Halloran says, bemused. "She's gone clear out of the state, in fact. Seems fishy."

"She had nothing to do with it, and you shouldn't—"

O'Halloran is making a note on the pad when Houston turns his angry gaze toward him, and he looks up then, gaze almost sheepish under his heavy eyelids, but refuses to repent. Houston picks his coat up and turns for the door.

"Detective, you said we were trading," O'Halloran reminds. "Don't you want the truth about the Winsome case to get out instead of a bunch of guesswork? It'll come out at trial, anyway, or enough for the prosecutor to try and get Winsome the chair."

"If *she* wanted it out, she'd talk to you about it," Houston says. "I'm done."

"Can you give me any other leads?" O'Halloran's voice raises after Houston's departing back, in that strident reporter's tone that Houston knows lifts his voice over the rest of the pack's.

He ignores it, stepping into his shoes without bothering to get on his socks, stuffing them balled up into his pocket and heading for the front door. He can't really hold it against O'Halloran, the man's dogged determination to get a lead is like his own in a lot of ways, except Houston doesn't air all that dirty laundry outside his own backyard.

Outside, the cold air welcomes Houston back into it, like he's kin. He takes a minute to rake his hand through his hair, pushing the disarray out of it as if it were as easy to smooth his life back into alignment after O'Halloran's greedy fingers had unmade all the order in it.

A low black car pulls up, parking alongside the curb in the street in front of O'Halloran's house, and Houston is at first too distracted by the chill curling around his ankles as he makes his way down the porch stairs with his eyes trained for a bus-stop to recognize the bulky figure filling the driver's side seat.

Then the man gets out, unfolding himself up to a full, solid height that catches Houston's attention away from the bus-stop sign he's charting his course by, and for a moment, their eyes meet and Houston feels every sin that's just transpired, every sodomy law he just broke like they were all painted on his skin and screaming out.

Halward Exeter's eyes are stone-hard on Houston, like he knows what Houston's just done, senses it like a bloodhound can sniff it with his good cop's instincts, like the blood they both spilled together in the end of the previous year gives them some connection beyond the begrudging respect they owe each other.

He stares at Houston for a long moment, then up at O'Halloran's house, and then Ex tears his gaze away and looks anywhere else but, pretending to be busy until Houston clears out of the area.

3.

Houston's fishing in his pocket for the bus fare when he remembers Sal, and guilt for his betrayal—done in a desperately casual fashion—floods over him like ice water.

Hell, Houston thinks, dropping the change into the counter with heavy-sounding thunks that mirror the way his insides suddenly feel. *It's not like we have anything official.*

It's a poor excuse for his rashness, for the way both of them have left the shared part of their life in limbo for so long. There used to be a bright spark between them whenever Sal's smile put flint to that tinder. Houston's not sure he can ignore that, or convince himself what's between them is and has only ever been convenience.

Lately, the bright shine that was his light in the dark as he and Sal navigated their way through their previous years has tarnished over. It isn't a change in Sal, or the deeper relationship, or the way their minds and bodies fit together. It's the shadow of the past that hangs over all of that, a grim shroud covering the promise of the future, turning Houston away from it as if touching something he cared about now would sap all the color out of it.

He can feel the scrap of paper in his pocket like an anchor dragging him down, and he wrestles his thoughts away from his guilt and the need for immediate pursuit of the subject, instead thinking of the curious encounter he had at the end of his otherwise productive (for him) interview.

Halward Exeter, Houston thinks. He wonders if O'Halloran is also trying to get details of the Winsome case out of Ex. He hasn't seen the police detective since last year in the alley. Lucas' case was transferred to Detective Ward, and Houston went out of his way to avoid Exeter afterward.

There is still no love lost between them, even if they've come to understand each other a little better. Houston wonders if he still goes into the bar that cops frequent, and runs his mouth when the other officers pick on a Sally. Maybe his experiences have made him a little wiser. Either way, he hasn't reached out to Houston, either. By mutual agreement they've returned to their old enmity.

So, what was he doing at Dan O'Halloran's house? Houston wonders, as he sits down stiffly in one of the bus-seats and watches the slushy Chicago world revolve outside. His body is that pleasant kind of sore, and it brings up a new wave of guilt. *How the hell am I going to tell Sal?*

Houston's slow descent into the pit of his own obsession hasn't done them any favors. Indecision wars inside him and guilt drives him to check in at the office—see if Miss Wentz has anything for him, or if Sal left a note.

Even her alcove is empty, the little stool she sits on all day tucked tidily under the counter and the connection wires for the phone system neatly coiled and hung up. Houston hesitates, and then reaches for the headset, plugs in the outside line and asks for the operator in Los Angeles.

"One moment please, I'll get you connected through," a woman's voice, with a pleasant city-accent, the kind Houston's come to get used to as part of his daily existence, tells him. Houston waits as the line clicks and then rings.

"Los Angeles Primary Exchange," a different accent tells him. "How can I help you?"

"Ma'am, I have a Hollywood address and I was wondering if you could give me the number for the house, if there is one?" Houston asks, leaning his elbow up on Miss Wentz's desk.

"I'm sure willing to try, sir," she says, sounding falsely bright. "May I have the address please?"

Houston pulls the piece of paper out of his pocket, looking at O'Halloran's thin lettering, and wonders if he should get rid of it after this. As he relays the address to the operator, he fishes around for a pen or a pencil in his pocket, finally resorting to pulling open Miss Wentz's drawer and taking one of hers for the duration of the note.

"There's no individual lines in that complex, sir, but there's a main office phone for the development."

"May I have that, please?"

"That's Stanley exchange, number seventy-eight," she says. "I'll put you through and the girl there can connect you, if you'd like?"

"Please, ma'am, thank you," Houston says, making an annotation with his borrowed pen. On the other end of the line there are clicks and rings again, and then another woman takes his request and connects his wire—funny to think four feet of cable could cover all the distance from Chicago to California.

The line rings and rings, going on and on. Houston listens to it repeat ten times before the operator comes back on the line.

"I'm sorry sir, no one's answering," she says.

"That's alright," Houston says, folding the paper back up and returning it to his pocket. "Thank you for your time."

The Sappho greets Houston with a wheezing, sad blues sound, as he enters from the cold early spring evening air into the tired grandeur of the place. It's not aging gracefully, but the faded image of Baccus waits, saluting him.

Gone are the crowds of the twenties, daring and gay with drink. Houston sees that the men inside have become islands, save for the old timer's table and the group of musicians making jazz from their cluster on the raised stage. There's a saxophone case sitting open at the edge of the stage, containing a paltry handful of change and a few soft rags for the care of the instruments.

Houston scrapes a dime out of his pocket and tosses it in a gentle arc into the musician's case.

The piano player—a drag dresser in the performing style of the recently meteoric Julian Eltinge—gives him a nod and an expert coquettish wink. She looks tired under her flawless makeup. Another facade that's fading under pressure. She's pretty anyway, Houston thinks, in the objective way he finds any woman pretty.

He finds a seat to occupy, setting his heavy body into one of the many empty chairs at the empty tables scattered around the main room. Houston's not sure he could say what's brought him if anyone asks; some desire to fold time? To return to his nights spent here with Lucas? He wants to feel close to Lucas again, close to who he himself was, back then. He needs to understand a lot of things about this, and he feels the years between him and Lucas like a cliff face in his thoughts.

At the time, Houston thought Lucas' capricious nature was a key quality for his survival. It was just easier not to get bogged down in pain or fear. To forget that it was dangerous for men of their persuasion in the world around them. It was easy for Lucas —and *around* Lucas.

Houston watches life in the Sappho go by for a little while, until a tired-looking waitress comes around to take his order.

"What are you *having*?" she leans a little heavy on the emphasis, Houston gets the impression he's got to pay if he wants to stay.

"What're my options?" he asks, without real enthusiasm. He'd take a whiskey, but if they still have any in some secret cubby, he's not enough of a regular anymore to get it if he asks.

"Soda—seltzer and lemon, coffee…" she lists. Houston hears all the hallmarks of a well-stocked bar ravaged by prohibition. Yet another place suffering under the thumb of the eighteenth amendment.

Between that and the Depression, Houston wonders if he should count the days until the Sappho closes her doors for good. For now, she's still holding out like one sad, empty lighthouse at sea.

"Coffee," Houston decides, after a glance at his wallet. "And a lemon seltzer."

"Keeps the scurvy away," the waitress intones drily, without bothering to even note his order down.

Houston suspects this place gets it share of deadbeats, in off the street for some warmth and a chance to wet their whistle. He's sorry he can't afford more, but at least he intends to pay.

The jazz plays on, touching all the long, blue notes in Houston's soul. He watches the other loners in the bar, all nervous-eyed and careful. Every so often, he sees an orbit collide—two men sit together, share a drink and dare to trust each other enough to be private together.

Houston recalls the first night he spent in this once-hallowed hall. He screwed up all of his courage to come. It was two weeks after he'd returned from the war.

He'd seen Lucas in a very popular stage show in the giddy time following armistice, as the twenties began to roar and before they came to to a fruition none of them expected. Maybe even then, before they'd met properly, Houston was already in Lucas' hold. He'd heard that Lucas—and the other actors in the production—frequented the Sappho, so Houston came. That night, as Houston sat alone waiting for a chance just to *see* the actors, Lucas swept in, grandiose as the lady Venus emerging from the sea.

The place came *alive* then, a pack of bodies so tight that Houston couldn't get away from his place at the bar, sitting shoulder to shoulder with a few other former soldiers. It wasn't a familiar scene for any of them, but the hollow-eyed curiosity of these men was been absorbed into the promise of booze and joyous company. An openness of conduct they'd so long had to hide that it seemed both callous and intoxicating to the men who'd had their last few hurried trysts in the blood and mud of the front, or a rabbit hole in a trench somewhere.

Then Lucas and the other actors swept through the crowd toward the bar, and in that instant something changed. It was like the death of fear, transcendence from the rest of the world's condemnation. After all, here were the stars—and everything Lucas touched seemed to become all music and ethereal light.

Houston went to them, as if drawn on puppet strings. When Lucas embraced him that night, it was an experience outside time.

In his absence, shame has moved back into the Sappho. Houston won't find any part of Lucas here anymore. He feels foolish to have come at all. The past is beyond his reach, and the future is out of sight.

Houston drinks his coffee slowly when his order comes, and the waitress doesn't even offer any sugar so he drinks it black. He watches the stage where the musicians play on, their enthusiasm slowly melting under the pressure of passing time and poor attendance. No other patrons come to Houston's table. He must give off the aura of someone untouchable these days. He's grateful. After his encounter earlier with Dan O'Halloran, he doesn't trust himself.

Absently, Houston wonders if Ex still comes in. *Has scandal chased him away from this place, too? What was he doing at O'Halloran's today?*

"So here's a question for the pulpit," a voice—*Sal's* voice, as if conjured out of Houston's guilt. His tone is sugared and low, meant for Huston's ears only. "If you can roust me out of my bad habits and call it a favor, is turnabout just petty revenge or an *obligation?*"

Houston looks up over his shoulder. He didn't see Sal come in, so he must have come down from the upstairs. A tingle of curiosity, with the faint and cynical flavor of jealousy (and hypocrisy) touches the back of Houston's neck.

"I'm not even drinking," Houston says, as Sal sits in the opposite chair. "Just chasing memories."

"For you, that's a vice," Sal says, on the razor's edge between serious and joking. "You cut yourself deeper than my smoke ever went."

Houston's not so sure, but he deflects Sal's barbs with a question instead. "What are you doing here, then? Not cruising?"

Sal produces his battered pack of cigarettes from his coat pocket and flags the waitress down for an ashtray. When he's lit and taken the first quarter of the cig to ash, he lets it burn in a notch of the ashtray while he talks. "I got a call today while you were out. A case that wanted sympathetic ears. Don't ask me how you got that reputation."

"What kind of sympathy?" Houston asks.

"The kind that has me meeting a client here," Sal says. "For a minute, after I got the call, I worried it was a bust setup—and that it was meant for *you*."

"You're paranoid," Houston says. The cigarette in the ashtray is slowly reducing itself before his starving eyes. "There's nothing to be gained by defaming me."

"They could get you off the stand in the Winsome case," Sal says. "Paranoia's how I lived through the trenches."

"Good sense wasn't it, if you're here anyway."

"*Funny!*" Sal intones. He picks up the cigarette again. "Two little voices in the back of my head got the better of me. One was saying something about making rent on my apartment and your office next month."

"*Our* office," Houston corrects. "What was the other voice?"

"Sounded like you. Kept saying things about how there's got to be justice for everybody. Even the people the cops don't like." Sal pauses, then offers his half-finished cigarette to Houston like a sort of peace offering. "Maybe *especially* the people the cops don't like."

Houston takes the offered cigarette, placing it between his lips and inhaling. It *does* sound like his voice, echoed back in Salvatore's dry, Italian-flavored Chicago accent. He studies the white-paper contrast against his skin, rolling the cigarette back and forth as he feels the smoke roil in his lungs.

"Well?" he asks Sal.

"Well, what?"

"What's the case, wiseass?"

Sal smiles, a victory written in the revealed points of his incisors. "You remember *The Modern Menagerie of Madame Butterfly*?"

Houston has to think about it. Then, he has it, the memory seizing him like a bouncer at a bar. He has an image of paying a few francs at a half shelled out Parisian boudoir, finding the inside hastily rearranged for a film to show. He remembers an audience of men—and some French women—trying not to meet each other's eyes as they found seats in the darkened space.

He remembers that the intertitles were in French, and his grasp on the language was barely enough to follow the playful and irreverent plot. A low, dirty feeling spike of excitement as a silver-toned man took a silver-toned dick in his mouth on screen, one of several sexual acts portrayed in well lit and stark clarity.

Houston shakes the memory off.

"Leave it to the French," Houston says, as if he hasn't brought himself to pleasure several times while considering the images in memory. "What about it?"

"Well, it left a hunger," Sal says, as if reading Houston's innermost thoughts. "There's been a slowly growing underground movement to make other films like it. A whole ring of people processing film in their bathtubs, and trying to keep the Mob out of it."

Houston's not surprised, exactly, but he feels disconnected. Years ago he's sure he would have been aware of this subculture. He observes, "Never a good idea to try and keep the Mafia out of money."

"Prohibition makes them richer every day. But they're real touchy about their image, too. Homosexual stuff—that's not a cut I really think they want."

"Alright, so what's the case?" Houston asks, piqued. He knows Sal's playing him for interest.

"A few weeks ago, the casting call goes out for willing guys," Sal says. "Through the usual word-of-mouth chain. Money's attached, apparently a significant offering."

"It's a dangerous profession."

"Uh huh," Sal says. "And it's dependant on new faces, new bodies. Collectors don't want essentially the same film over and over. And in times like these..."

Houston puts it together on his own. Desperate men, starving or seeing no hope of anything beyond what put a dollar in their pocket today. Willing to take a risk on what amounted to a couple of hour's pleasurable work. "Well, were they trying to recruit *you*, or what?"

"Hah!" Sal says. "No, but you know I might do it. Fame and fortune?"

"Be serious."

"It might pay better than this job. My dick *could* be a movie star."

Houston knows better than to disagree.

"No," Sal reveals. "The case is that all the guys—about fifteen of them—that answered this casting call are now missing. Gone about a month, now."

"Shit." Houston's gut goes south. *When will the first corpse turn up?*

"Yeah," Sal says. "We have one client on behalf of a few, looking for friends and loved ones. Mr. White is trying to get some solid lines on leads for us. The police got wind of what kind of trouble it is, and don't want anything to do with it."

"Shit."

"That's what I thought," Sal says. His tone is resigned but his eyes have the shine of a hound on the hunt.

And it'll be one hell of a fox they're after.

Houston and Sal part ways for the evening but the case turns over in Houston's thoughts while he rides the nearly empty last bus home. He realizes he's lost track of the day of the week, of the date. It's still March, anyway. It promises to be a slushy, unpleasant spring and the ice on the lakes doesn't seem to be going anywhere soon.

A boon for Sal's ice-box maybe.

At home, Houston thinks about moving pictures. About how everyone villainizes the pornographers and praises the Hollywood films that cover over their sins with what they show on celluloid and silver screen, rather than blatantly showing their steamy underside.

Maybe Houston has it wrong, too. Maybe the films are just as filthy, no matter what the audience is; after all, whether or not fornication was the subject, the emotional material was for sale. Whether it was laughter or longing or lust, a service humanity has been paying for since the rise of the Greek tragedy.

He feeds Chop Suey a half-and-half mix of canned Dr. Pross pet food and tuna fish. The cat considers the contents of the bowl, then Houston skeptically.

"Sorry it's not caviar, we're fresh out," Houston tells the cat. Chop Suey gives him a doubtful expression before finally deigning to eat only the tuna, green eyes glistening in the dim light of the kitchen.

Houston drops into his bed alone and he can still smell Sal's brand of cigarettes in his clothes and a faint trace of his coffee from the Sappho.

He wonders who the client is, realizes he hasn't asked Sal about the pay. Then, Chop Suey joins Houston in the bed, bringing with him a purr and a warm weight; the scent of tuna and horsemeat. He settles in beside Houston and closes his luminous eyes when Houston rubs his stubby ears.

Sal's old clunker is waiting at the corner when Houston comes down his apartment stairs in the morning. The concrete is swept bare of slush carefully, a ritual that the tenants of Houston's building have taken up after a ten year old broke his arm right on the heels of Houston's accident the prior winter.

Houston doesn't have the heart to tell them that his fall probably saved his life—he likes not slipping and tracking slush in every time he approaches the building.

Sal is wrapped in a blanket and waiting for him behind the wheel. Houston approaches, leaning on the driver's side and considering how he feels about this intense babysitting. "You're up early."

"So are you," Sal answers, giving Houston a sly look from under the brim of his hat. For all Houston's mooning around over long lost love, he can still appreciate Sal's good looks.

"I usually get up early," Houston reminds. "But it takes an act of God to get you to work by *ten*."

"When we don't have a case, there's hardly a reason to get up before nine anyway. Do you want a ride to work or to stand around jawing until we're *both* late?"

Houston settles into the passenger seat of Sal's hayburner and leans back, wondering if this is honest work ethic on Sal's behalf or close supervision of Houston under another guise. Sal's idea of taking care of his wayward friend.

"So I didn't ask last night," Houston starts as Sal pulls into the street. "But what are we getting paid for this case? Guys who are that desperate for an audition probably don't have the money to pay a retainer."

"Good thing we ain't lawyers," Sal says.

"We don't have money for operating expenditures out of pocket," Houston protests. "Sal, we can't do this for free."

"We aren't," Sal says, with faint reassurance. "But I took it out in trade."

"On *what*?"

"You wanna work this case or you wanna go back to moping about your past? 'Cause you weren't making anything on what you were doing before except a lot of regret. If that's the wages you want to collect…"

Houston feels a fresh pang of guilt wash over him, like the last traces of O'Halloran's cologne on Houston's shirt collar before he put it in the laundry bag. They've come a long way since Sal's sobriety has really set in. He used to prefer to avoid any confrontation, and now he's trapped Houston neatly in one.

"Sometimes, you just have to." Houston can hear how tired his own voice sounds.

"Well," Sal says. "Now we have two things we *have to*."

The office is chilly when they get to it, and Houston goes to get coffee on and gives the radiator a crank as they settle in for a work day. Sal produces a battered notepad from his inner pocket, displaying a sheet of his scratchy handwriting to Houston, who can't make heads or tails of his unofficial pidgin shorthand. It seems to be an address, or some of it is, anyway.

"Sal, you gotta take a course," Houston says, pushing the notepad back at him. "I can't read this."

Accepting his notebook back, Sal considers it as if a close scrutiny will make his handwriting more legible. "You should have your eyes checked."

"A set of prescription lenses would just make it *big* and unreadable."

"So the details are as such," Sal settles into the chair opposite Houston's desk and pulls his cup of coffee toward him after Houston pours it. "An address for a place in Levytown was circulated and interested parties were supposed to turn up at four-thirty in the afternoon on the sixteenth of February."

"Alright, you have the address?" Houston asks, unsure why they came all the way to the office if they had the information to hit the streets already.

"Yes. It's not too far from the Sappho, but no place you want to be hanging around alone after dark."

"Hence the early meet time," Houston says.

"Well, in February, that's almost dark."

"Who spread the word? We got an origin?"

"It's all *heard it from a guy who heard it from some other guy*," Sal says. "That, in and of itself, is not unusual."

"Protects the source."

"But I guess these guys usually have some inkling of an origin. There's an in-town ring, some known operators. Nobody talks about it, but better the devil you know, that sort of thing."

"Not this time?"

"These were out-of-towners," Sal confirms. "Gave—or at least did not dissuade—the impression that they were real Hollywood types."

Broadening the net and sweetening the bait, Houston thinks. "Don't people know the lines don't cross?"

"Houston, what man knows anything in his heart that he won't doubt when money, love, or sex is involved?" Sal asks, philosophically.

"Not a one." Houston can hardly do other than agree without extreme hypocrisy.

"Anyway, the names I got were only for missing men. Nobody got names on the big shot out-of-towners, of course."

"If they were up to no good, they used aliases anyway," Houston guesses. "So why didn't we go straight there? Is there anything permanent at the address?"

"An old office building," Sal says. "They'll rent by the week, no questions. Which also means no answers."

"You've spoken to them?"

"Not yet. You think that's an avenue worth pursuing?"

"What were you planning on tracking down first?" Houston asks. Sal picked the case up; technically it's his initiative to work it. He hasn't been a detective long, but Sal has good instincts, if somewhat lazy tendencies.

"I thought we could check the theater where the guy saw the stag film," Sal says. "Talk to the guy who orchestrated the viewing and see where he got the film. Then we talk to that guy. Somewhere in that chain of custody somebody knows something."

"The question is if they'll tell *us* what they know."

"Oh ye of little faith," Sal says. "They'll tell us."

The building has seen better days. It's a run down dump in a land of run down dumps that's remarkable only for its one-time color. It has, still, a gaudy red facade that leaves little doubt as to the nature of the place. The electrically powered bulb under the red-glass lantern that stands out from the front of the boxy building is no longer functioning.

Houston puts his cigarette out on the pavement and tries to remember if he's ever laid eyes on this place before. If he has, it was in such a state of intoxication that he doesn't recall.

The building is chipping all over; paint, bricks, wood frontage. It was once meant to emulate the saloons of the old wild west —porched in windows at the top floor, where perhaps, in the prosperous era after the war, ladies of the night had lounged and beckoned men in, fresh off the boats home. Now they're in disrepair, dismal and rotted wood. Houston despairs of the integrity of the whole second floor.

"Is anyone here today?" he asks Sal.

"Should be. What kind of whorehouse is ever empty?" Sal wonders. "It's not like they have a number down here so they can schedule appointments."

"Not exactly a priority to run the phone lines down here."

He follows Sal into the boudoir's front door, unable to help giving a surreptitious look around at the street before he steps in. *As if my reputation could really get any worse,* he thinks, realizing what he's done.

It's dark inside, lit by glass enclosed candles in a narrow entry hall that puts Houston in mind of some of the corridors with murder holes in ancient castles he saw while overseas. The flowery, once-vibrant wallpaper tries to crowd an implication of cheerfulness against his shoulders. It does nothing to decrease the oppressive feeling.

"Hello?" Sal calls into the interior. He proceeds up the hall to where a bored looking matron is reading a less-than-savory-looking novel behind a low desk.

She's a bigger woman, squeezed into a corset that tames her body into a false curvature which puts emphasis on her bosom —ample, but otherwise shapeless. Houston worries for her comfort, but supposes from her easy and slumping posture that she is—if not comfortable—at least used to it. She rolls mud-colored eyes up at the pair of them.

"You two want a girl or just a room?" she asks, sticking a ticket scrap—an old, weathered piece of brown paper that says 'admit one'—into her novel and turning to them with her hands folded together and an expectant look on her face.

"We'd like to talk to you," Sal says, leaning on the counter like he's unphased by her divination. He turns on the charm, easing into a slouching posture that displays a relaxed guard while he smiles at her.

"That's not on the menu," she says, giving them both the hairy eyeball.

"We're not here for the menu," Sal assures her. "We want to ask about a movie we heard was playing up here a week ago."

"We only do one showing," the matron says, looking between

Houston and Sal like they're a fine pair of morons. "It's a hush-hush affair, fellas. I have no idea when the next fairy film will fly through."

"We don't want to know about the next one," Houston keeps his tone polite. "I know a collector, he'd like a copy for his personal collection."

Sal doesn't miss a beat. "We were wondering if you knew where the film came from."

"Came from a couple of clowns who still think people have the energy to shake one out to movies," the matron says. "A couple of clowns like *you* would fit right in."

"Say, I don't think she likes us," Sal says, trading a mock-stung look with Houston.

"I think you two look like you haven't got two dimes to rub together," she says.

She's not wrong, but Houston figures he can probably talk past that. "What would you like in exchange for the phone number of those clowns who brought you the film?"

She looks at the both of them like they're aliens. "That's not how this works. The films come in. We run them once, and then they go out."

"So if I walked in with a film tomorrow, you'd play it?" Sal presses.

"You two better leave now," she says. "I'm wasting my time with you."

The feeling is mutual, Houston thinks.

"We're just asking for some names," Sal tries, but Houston sees she's not going to budge.

"I'm telling you," the matron says, reaching under her desk in a way that draws Houston's eye. "We got no use for people who come around asking strange questions. No use for cops, either."

"We aren't—" Sal starts. Houston puts a hand on his arm, steadying him.

"We aren't after trouble, ma'am," Houston continues to hold onto his polite tone. "Just information. Let me leave my card, okay?"

He folds the last ten dollar bill in his wallet beneath it, and figures he'll go without something for the month. She takes the card and the bribe and doesn't promise anything.

"If these folks come back through with another film, we'd appreciate a call," Houston says, relieved to see her hand lower from beneath the desk back to her lap. Whether she had her hand on an alarm or a gun, Houston doesn't ever want to find out.

He guides Sal out, back into the cool air.

"Think you just gave away a good chunk of change for nothing?" Sal asks.

"Made a wager," Houston says. "She strikes me as the protective type. Maybe word gets back to her about the missing folks. Maybe she has questions about why we were here."

Sal pulls a pack of Lucky Strikes out of his pocket, shaking one free. He puts the extended cigarette to his mouth and eases it free between his teeth. "Maybe."

Houston tosses him some matches. "What's the next step?"

A strike fills the cool air with the scent of sulfur and the faint glow of flame as Sal delays his answer while he lights the cigarette. "Office building?"

"Can't hurt." Houston says. At the least, it would be no worse than their bust on the surface, and there's a part in the back of his mind that's aware of time passing, of how many people who are potentially stuck in this twisted machine and relying on them, and probably *only* them.

He and Sal head back toward the car, and Houston pauses at a light pole, looking over the dozens of stapled up flyers for any sign. They're carefully worded, avoiding any promises of out-right pornography, but they get close.

"Anything catch your fancy?" Sal asks, as Houston joins him in the car.

"These days I don't think I fancy much of anything," Houston admits, running his eyes over the neighborhood. "It all reminds me of how desperate things were in the war."

"That's just the economy talking."

"If you're starving in a tent behind trench lines, or you're starv-ing in the street, you're still starving."

"Guess so," Sal says. In the air between them, something lingers unsaid but neither of them moves to change that.

They chase the case for a week before Houston's straying thoughts betray him. For all he's aware of the clear and present danger, he wants to know more about what O'Halloran said. About what drove Lucas to his final death, put him in an alley-way in Chicago when by all rights he should have been in Los An-geles, still working on shining up his star.

Had film eaten his life up, called him in desperate to make it, convinced of his talent and worth only to catch him up in a net like the men in the skin flicks? What if it was a common scheme out there where the cameras were plentiful and it's crept across the country like a greedy hunter now, seeking more meat for the table?

If he goes to California, will he be able to see Lucas' ghost on the big screen? The empty, naked shell of him laid out like a silver idol made for sacrifice?

The odds of that are unlikely. It's a bad gamble, and yet the idea refuses to depart from Houston's thoughts, catching and holding on like a blood sucking insect. He sleeps poorly, waking in the nights to his lone apartment with dozens of scenarios playing out in his thoughts.

Why hadn't he gone looking *sooner*? Could he have prevented this? And, a quieter, more sinister part of himself asks, *would I have wanted to?* Lucas' disappearance left an open wound inside Houston. The quiet internal bleeding he saw take men silently on the battlefield. *Isn't this final resolution actually a relief?*

Houston knows that if at any point, Lucas had tried to re-enter his life, he'd have let him in. Unhesitantly, unreservedly opened the door and let the stitches he'd put on the straight-razor slash in his own heart be pulled out.

You're a fool, you're doing it to yourself anyway, Mars, Houston admonishes himself as he tosses over on his bed.

An inky black shape shifts next to him, and Chop Suey comes awake, disturbed by Houston's restlessness. He blinks his green eyes at Houston in feline displeasure, then shifts to lay over Houston's chest to weigh him down and reassure him.

It feels stifling.

4.

Two days later as they enter the building, Miss Wentz calls after them. "Mr. Costanzo, you have a message."

"Hey, lookit that," Sal leans in to take the canary-yellow slip of paper from Miss Wentz, smiling at her in a way that makes her own grin answer. "Thank you, Katie."

"Of course. I hope it breaks your case!" She turns her grin on Houston. "Aren't you working it, too?"

"Uh-huh," Sal answers on his behalf. "It's slow going. We got anything else waiting?"

"No, sir," Miss Wentz says, offering a twinkling and apologetic smile. "Been real slow these last few days. Why, I've almost read this whole book just waiting for a line to buzz."

Houston supposes the newspapers haven't been calling, with the initial pre-trial testimony from last Thursday to chew over and digest. Seems like there's something new in the papers every day. Whatever attorney the state has assigned to Arthur Winsome Jr. hasn't managed to impress on him not to run his mouth.

"Thanks, Miss Wentz," Houston says. "Buzz up if there's an evening edition for us, won't you?"

She smiles, nodding, and turns back around on her stool to pick her book back up.

"Hey," Sal says, as they chug their way up the stairs. "Did you notice? She didn't call you Huey even once."

"She didn't call me anything."

"That's a start, isn't it?"

Houston wonders when it was that Sal became the optimistic one. He supposes that's in the nature of their relationship—each of them swinging in pendulum time to keep the balance, keep things functional. Maybe that's how everything has to work in a depression, on a weighed scale of momentum and rebound.

In the office, Houston turns on the lights, fires up the electric burner under the percolator. Sal turns on the Victrola, quietly, and Cab Calloway's voice growls out fast time but soul-sad and worth a million bucks. Houston measures the last fresh coffee grounds from the can into the percolator.

"What's it say?" he asks at last, finding Sal still in his office chair, behind the desk covered in scattered, disorganized papers. He still has the yellow slip in hand, a lit cigarette in the other up by his temple in the modern man's thinking pose.

"It's a lead," Sal says, with a shrug. "I think we'd better talk to Mr. White. Seems like he's caught his missing man on another film last night."

"At the same place?"

"We'll have to ask," Sal says, displaying the scant note in Miss Wentz's hand.

S. Costanzo—Saw a film last night. Have information about one of the missing men, and about sets used. Afterwards, a number and address are listed.

Houston feels his interest pique up. "We should look into this."

"That's what detectives do," Sal agrees. "Call or go?"

Houston can smell the freshly brewed coffee calling out its dramatic promise for wakefulness. He sighs and knows what the appropriate answer is. He rinses out his mug and fills it with coffee to go before he turns off the pot. "We go. It's always better to see someone face to face."

Sal leaves his cigarette half finished in the ashtray and joins Houston in putting his coat back on.

Erwin White agrees to meet them at his place—lakeside. It's a once-grand house now crumbling, teetering on rocks and raise-poles and waiting for a storm to come pull the drunkard's legs out from under it and wash it away at last.

"Come and see my shining castle built upon the sand," Sal mutters, as they climb out of his car.

"Palace," Houston corrects offhandedly.

"Huh?"

"It's 'palace built upon the sand'."

"Huh." Sal lights a cigarette, cupping the flame against the lake wind. "Guess I always think of sand castles."

"Didn't take you for much of a poetry person, anyway."

Gravel crunches underfoot as it did under the car tires. The pathway is slushy—pea-gravel and crushed shell under snow. No way to shovel it; it reminds him of a dozen winters at home, his older brother pulling a scraping sled over the walkways with firewood while Houston struggled to keep up in waist-deep snow.

Sal takes the lead on the porch, tapping snow from his shoes at the bottom of the steps, which are carefully cleared. White opens the door at the top, and looks down at them through spectacles.

Houston's first impression is that Mr. White is dressed shabbily, but in comfortable clothes that fit him well, a trim cream-corded sweater over dove gray slacks. He looks more like a college professor than the usual dirty-movie haunts. Houston supposes he doesn't know anything about what the average pornography patron looks like these days. He hasn't been since the war.

"Good morning, detectives," Erwin says, in a soft voice. To Houston's eye, he has the mild presence of a discreet career homosexual. Houston has known several such men, supposes he'll be one someday.

They step into the parlour, and Houston's suspicions are confirmed by the decor. The family photos are far too old to indicate anyone other than Mr.White lives here. The decor is sparse and carefully impersonal. Houston bets nothing has changed inside since Mr. White inherited the house from the parents in the photos.

"Good morning, Mr. White," Sal introduces. "I'm Salvatore Costanzo, this is my partner, Houston Mars."

Houston offers his hand as he's expected to. Mr. White's grip is soft, but present and his hands are paper dry. Houston wonders about this narrow view into the man's life, and how the seeming safety of it has intersected with such a terrifying corner of the world.

"We have some questions about the information you left with our secretary," Sal says.

"Of course you do," White says, genially, with just a hint of worry. The 'fear of the worst' that's been common to all walks of life these days. "I do too. Will you have some coffee?"

"Yes, thank you," Houston says, almost exactly in concert with Sal.

"Come sit down," White says, inviting them into his kitchen. "Your secretary is a lovely girl, by the way. Very sweet, and so cheerful! I didn't know people could work on the phone and hang onto their good manners."

The space in the kitchen is warmer, the percolator on the stove and the scent of coffee filling the air. Houston and Sal each accept a weathered blue cup full of coffee that was better than the brew back at the office. Mr. White gestures for them to take a seat at the kitchen table.

"She loves the phone," Houston says, making a note to pass the compliment on to Miss Wentz. "And talking on it, but she's a nice girl at heart."

"You said you knew the set," Sal presses, into the soft pause at the conclusion of the previous subject, lunging for the meat of things. "Is it here in Chicago?"

"Oh, no," White says, his spoon clinking rhythmically in his cup. "That's in L.A."

"California?" Sal asks, checking with Houston in a glance, as if Houston might have some insight into what L.A. could mean aside from Los Angeles.

"Of course," White says. "The cameras are all there. Easier to move the talent to the cameras for something like that."

Makes sense to Houston in some ways. "So, they recruit from Chicago and shoot in Hollywood?"

"They used to—the old Selig Polyscope place here in Chicago, with a link to their studio in Edendale. Like every country girl dreams," White says, turning his coffee cup slowly on the table. "Anyway they only had one set. They redress it. This time, they *barely* did."

"Can you give us an address?" Sal asks.

Houston sips his coffee and watches for a response—any sign of aversion. Mr. White's pleasant school-teacher face betrays nothing but bland consideration.

"I'm struggling to remember," he says. "It was a while ago."

"How long?" Sal presses.

"Oh, years," White says. "Before the stock market went bust. The pictures—oh, well, a little high and mighty to call them 'pictures'..."

White hesitates a little, shifting uncomfortably in his seat.

"It's alright, Mr. White," Houston says. "We're not looking for evidence to incriminate anyone."

"I'm not sure I can give you what you *are* looking for," White says, looking up from his untouched coffee cup. "But I've been hoping that any little bit will help. I hate to see anyone go through what I did."

"I've been asking around with some of the other people you mentioned and there are some other disappearances that seem tied into these pornographic films," Sal says. "You said you knew one of the men, but hadn't heard from him in a while?"

"Jack," White says, nodding. "He's been unreachable for a while... I've been worried."

Houston understands too well. After the economy collapsed, all the people teetering on the edge fell off.

"Then I saw him in that movie yesterday," White continues. There's a faint tone of desperation in White's voice, as if he's willing the statement to be the truth. "I guess he made out okay."

"Not an old film?" Houston asks. "Any chance it could have been shot a while ago and only released now?"

"I don't think so," White says. "They *said* it was new, last night at that theater."

"And you're really sure it was... you said his name is Jack?" Sal presses. "They don't usually show any faces."

"Yes, I'm sure," Erwin says. He taps a spot above his collar bone demonstratively. "My younger brother has a port wine stain there. It's pretty distinctive."

Houston hadn't expected that information, and he quickly pulls his notepad out to write things down. It's quiet for a moment, while Houston gathers his thoughts and makes notes. "Has he ever been in a film like this before?"

White shakes his head emphatically. "He shouldn't need to be, either."

"Do you know how long after production these films make it to distribution?" Sal asks.

"Well, there's not a lot of work done on them in post. A little splicing and then they run a few copies... I'd say a couple months on the outside. Maybe as short as a week, if the audience isn't too discerning, or only one copy is made."

"This may be a stupid question," Sal says, and Houston reaches out to nudge him beneath the table, hoping to encourage him to sound more confident. Sal gives him an oblivious glance before continuing, "Why would only one copy be made?"

"Well, in most circumstances it's for a private collection. Folks who are very rich arrange it between themselves for whatever reason," White says. "But that's not always the case. Some of these execs—or producers—or whatever you call them take advantage of desperate young actors and actresses. They make one copy of a film and bank on it. Like a war bond."

"How's it pay off?" Houston asks. "And how do they get these kids to do it?"

"Money is the great motivator, these days," White says, sadly. "It used to be they'd tell the hopefuls that the film was only for a private collection, they'd just neglected to mention it was *theirs*, or they'd promise a breakout role in a real picture. Maybe throw in some cocaine to make it seem like a good idea. Now, they just have to offer money."

"Nobody has it, everybody needs it," Houston agrees. "How's it work on the turnaround?"

"More often than not it doesn't," White says. "But they sometimes have a film stashed and that somebody on the film gets to be somebody."

"Blackmail," Sal puts together.

"Sure. Hollywood stars will pay a lot—have a lot *to* pay—to keep their image clean," White reveals. "Anyway, to bring it all around again, that racket used to be run by T.J. Williams, but I've heard he's gone legit."

"Getting back to the studio," Houston prompts, trying to stir things in a different direction. "Where in L.A. is it?"

"It was a while ago," White repeats. "I remember it wasn't *on* Hollywood Boulevard, but it wasn't far. It wasn't too far from Selig Polyscope in Edendale, and I think Williams liked that."

"You met him?" Sal asks, prodding gently in the right direction.

"Detective Costanzo, the story I've been telling you is the one of my own life," White explains sadly. "After I saw my first movie, I fell in love. I was younger, stupider. I saw those beautiful stars and thought I belonged with them."

White turns his eyes away, taking in the faded and scraped black and white tile, set in big checkerboard patterns. In that moment, Houston realizes white's younger than he'd first guessed. He just seems to have given up on youth and the optimistic pursuits it brings.

"I shot the dirty film," White continues. "But I never got the promised part in any legitimate one. So they eventually called me two years ago, right after the crash, those vultures. They were as desperate as everybody else, I guess, and the bones hadn't started hitting the ground for them to pick."

"What'd they want?" Sal asks, gently. "You had no movie career."

"He threatened to show the film—or... he said he'd tell my wife." White looks up with the fierce, time-worn anger of a revisionist, his normally mild tone gone tight and bitter. "I laughed! I had almost forgotten ever doing it. And, of course, the joke was on *them*. I've never been married."

Houston clarifies, "So you didn't pay?"

"No," White says, firmly. There is a hard look in his eyes, maybe a hint of pride. "Jack insisted I shouldn't when I asked him what to do, and they didn't have anything."

"Anything ever come of the fact you didn't?"

"A letter came in the mail a week later. It had a few frames of film in it, and a demand for $500 sent to a P.O. Box in Orange County," White says. "But I didn't respond and nothing else came after that. Maybe they *did* release the film, but I never saw it if that's the case."

"Is that why you go to the shows in Levytown?" Sal asks.

"Partly," White admits, after a long silence where he looks angrily at Sal for airing that insight into the open. "And partly because cheap thrills are the only thrills I can afford."

Sal laughs a little, smiling brilliantly at the end as he fights to keep from spilling over into more guffaws. "Ain't that the truth for everybody, Mr. White?"

It seems to break the tension at last. White finally lifts his coffee cup to his mouth and some of the desperate shame seems to leave him. Houston's not sure if that's the only passion he's possessed in some time. White seems to reach back into himself, and pull the mild facade he greeted them with back over his features.

"Mr. White," Houston says. "Do you still have the letter?"

"Well," he says, thinking. "Maybe, yes. I burned the film but I kept the letter. I didn't know what to do. Of course I couldn't go to the *police* with it. But I thought if things escalated, I might have to have something to show."

"If you have it, it might help us. Jack could be in trouble, and there's some other folks missing that it might help."

"Let me go and see," White says. He gets up from the table, pausing to set the coffee pot on the table for them. "Help yourselves while you wait, gentlemen. Hopefully it won't take too long."

Sal gets up, "Do you mind if I—"

"If you want to smoke, please do it outside," Mr. White requests. "I can't abide the smell when it's stale."

"Of course. I'll be out on the porch just there," Sal says, and they both go separate ways down the hall, leaving Houston to finish his cup in reflective silence. He refills it from the pot before he joins Sal outside in the chill.

"I wonder whoever thought of putting sex on film for the first time?" Sal wonders, as Houston lights up a Chesterfield.

"Probably the same guy who thought up the zoetrope," Houston says. "Pictures of sex are as old as pictures. Ask the Greeks."

He only realizes how unsteady his nerves are when he pulls the first lungfull of smoke. The whole situation is rotten and it churns Houston's stomach. Blackmail is bad enough, bribing people with their own naked bodies—especially those stars that already seem to have sold all their other privacies by contract—leaves him feeling cold and ill.

"Why'd you kick me?"

Houston drags his thoughts for context, before it comes up from the depths. "You doubted your own question."

"So?"

"So," Houston lays the points down with ticking fingers, unfolding the index first. "If you want answers, your questions have to be important, which means you gotta *ask* like they're important."

"How do I know which ones are important?"

"You don't, which is why you ask every question like it is. Sometimes even offhand stuff is critical. Folks will relate more of it to you if they think you're really listening."

"What about people who are trying to figure out what's important to withhold?" Sal asks.

"If you ask all the questions like they're important, those guys go for a loop. If someone's holding out on you, start asking left field questions like there's nothing else on your mind. Where you last friday? How do you take your coffee?"

"Does that really work?"

"Sure," Houston says. "Most of the time."

"Gentlemen?" White's voice calls from inside the house. "I found it."

When they're back on the road again, Houston examines the envelope in his hands. It's folded once but not often handled. No return address, but the stamp has a postal code emblazoned over it. Houston bets it goes to L.A., maybe outside the city but not too far.

There's a typewritten address on the front; bold, black, and unsmudged. From a fresh typewriter tape. The letter inside is the same.

"A professional," Houston says, after examining it.

"Well, Mr. White seems to think it's a whole racket," Sal answers, glancing over at what Houston's doing.

"Yeah, but even old-hands can get complacent. This guy used a fresh tape in his typewriter."

"Even if it wasn't two years old, what's that matter?"

"I bet he sent a whole slew in one day. One tape's worth. Drop the letters, burn the tape. No record."

"How's he remember where to follow up?" Sal wonders.

"Either a little black book or a big personal memory. My bet's on encoded notes."

"Sure, an operation like this is a lot of work. Gotta know who you have a reel of, where they are now."

Houston agrees. *Seems like a lot for a one-person operation, but maybe for a careful net-fisherman…. He throws out the bait and even if only some come back, it's a big enough catch.*

"Maybe for most little fish, there isn't any follow-up," Houston says, tucking the letter into his suit pocket and bundling the blanket in his lap tighter around his hands. "White said nothing ever came of it when he didn't pay up."

"He also really didn't have anyone to follow up the threat with, either," Sal points out. "Maybe that's why."

"He has a job. Neighbors. Nobody's completely untouchable."

"So they make the threats and some people pay, some people don't, but some is enough."

"Like tuna fish," Houston agrees. He sighs. "Or at least it was two years ago. Seems like kidnapping is a step up from toothless blackmail."

"Maybe toothless blackmail is a step down if they usually go for movie stars."

"Maybe."

They make the rest of the way back to the office in thoughtful silence. Houston is glad to leave the chill of the car behind.

"I should check who had the P.O. box registered," Sal says.

"It'll be long since inactive," Houston warns.

Sal swings the door open, and warm air rushes out of the foyer to meet them, signalling Houston's body to shiver. He steps into the entry hall behind Sal.

"Good afternoon, Mr. Costanzo!" Miss Wentz calls cheerfully, leaning out of the phone alcove as they pass. She smiles at Houston, too. "No more messages, I'm afraid."

"That's alright," Sal answers. "We're pretty deep in it."

"Big case?" she asks.

"Every case is big these days," Sal returns and they head up the narrow, groaning stairs to the third floor.

"She didn't call you Huey," Sal offers, holding the door for Houston.

"Two strikes," Houston says. "Once more and I'll believe it's stuck."

"He's still in operation," Sal says, penetrating the haze that had rapidly settled around Houston on his return.

"What?" Houston asks, looking up from his desk.

"Jesus, Mars, are you into those news clippings again?"

Sal stands in the doorway of Houston's office with papers in his hands and his eyes trained on the array of articles spread over Houston's desk. Houston hastily covers up the address he got from Dan O'Halloran, as if he could hold his guilt at bay.

"All that talk about L.A. reminded me," Houston says, gathering the clippings together and tucking them into a drawer, out of sight of his partner's ire.

"Yeah?"

'Nevermind," Houston says. "What've you got?"

"T.J. Williams," Sal says. "He's got an office in L.A., still. Some kind of production service."

"You think he's still running the racket?"

"On the outside it looks up-and-up. Real movies seem to come out of the place. Mostly westerns shot on the Paramount lot."

"Sounds a little fishy to me."

"Given his past? It's downright hinky."

"So what do you figure is the real story?" Houston wonders, adjusting the ashtray on his desk.

"Someone picked up his debts," Sal says. "Changed the cover operation, and bought stock in his future."

Houston turns that over in his thoughts, quiet for a short time as he works out the most likely culprit. "He couldn't keep the Mob out."

"Sure. Getting tough for any smart, independent crook to stay unincorporated these days."

Houston sits back to digest this. He's not sure what the pair of them can hope to accomplish. If the Mafia claims you as an asset, there isn't a whole lot a private eye could do about it, except negotiate a ransom, perhaps.

"Did Mr. White offer to pay us?" Houston asks. "I didn't think to ask him, since you handled the start of the case. We're getting into the weeds, now. Going any further..."

The image of Lucas laying against the wall in the snow, of the sheet sliding back to reveal his face instead of Sal's and the numb feeling of cold that seems to come back to him even now gives Houston pause. Some part of it drags at him, even now. The corruption that is still eating men and women alive out there.

"Yeah, gonna need some capital," Sal says. "I'll call tomorrow and see what he wants to do. Maybe he can pass the hat, I know there's other folks out there missing people."

"Tomorrow?"

"Yeah," Sal says, as if it's obvious why. When Houston doesn't follow, Sal leans against the door frame, crossing his arms over his chest with a softening expression. "Hobbes, it's after five. We should go home."

"Yeah," Houston glances at his watch to verify, then rouses himself. "Guess I lost track of time."

Sal vanishes from the shore of Houston's doorway like a wave receding, then reappears after a moment, pulling on his coat. "You want a ride home?"

"I'll catch the six o'clock bus," Houston says, feeling heavy and weighted to his chair.

Sal hesitates a minute, as if deciding whether or not to protest. Finally, he grumbles, "Not tonight, Josephine."

He recedes again, and a few seconds later, Houston hears the outer door close.

5.

Houston has harbored a mistrust of airplanes since he was last been shipped out with the medical reserve, a long journey "over there" that left him starkly anxious, aware of every abnormal jolt and change of altitude.

During the war he saw them fall out of the sky, shot to ribbons and dropping like he always felt they should. Men are not meant to fly, not this way. In the years since, they've begun to market commercial flights, cheerful comfortable things where someone would come and sit with you if you were nervous. Drinks are served.

Houston eschews this when he makes his sudden departure from Chicago, favoring the train station instead. The Grand Central station has a massive waiting room with vaulted ceilings, and a marble floor, a brightly lit celebration of the ages past when anybody could afford to travel. Finding himself here, Houston wonders what his purpose really is.

It's a Saturday, and the station creeps and crawls with the remains of busy transit. He'd parted ways with Sal yesterday evening after finishing out the week with only uncooperative witnesses and empty leads. There's one thing left in Houston's mind to pursue. Houston looks up at the train boards, thinking along the lines of the transcontinental railroad.

Am I really going to chase this all the way to L.A.? he wonders, feeling over the lump of his wallet. He has no suitcase and there's not much in his wallet, only enough in his checking account for rent at the end of the month. It's a crazy, cockamamie idea that Houston can't conscionably pursue, and yet here he stands, the product of a twenty minute bus-ride from his apartment.

"Hey Mars," a voice interrupts his thoughts, and Houston feels irritation slide down his spine like a hot poker over lake-ice, leaving a trail of runoff that he wants to shake from his hide like a dog with a wet coat.

"What are you doing here, Ex?" Houston asks, without looking around. "Got some traveling to do?"

"I could ask you the same thing," Exeter answers, stepping up beside Houston, square shoulders filling his coat. He's not carrying a suitcase either, Houston notices. His overcoat looks a little heavy for the weather, even this far north.

"It's the first day of spring," Houston observes.

"Yeah well, *tomorrow* I'll get out my spring jacket," Exeter says, even-toned. "What are you doing here, Mars?"

"Contemplating a train-ride," Houston says. "I hear the warm weather comes early in sunny California."

"Shit," Exeter swears. "This is about that damn dead actor."

Houston turns around then at last, looking at Exeter for a clue as to why he's here. No suitcase, no timetable. *Is he following me?* The idea stabs a line of heat into Houston's gut, leaving him angry.

"I'm curious what it was you *though*t it was about," Houston says.

"I thought maybe that rat O'Halloran was trying to out you," Exeter says. "Maybe you were running away."

Houston eases back on his heels, reaching for sense in Exeter's words. While Houston was there, in the reporter's presence, he was sure that the scam he'd run to get Houston back to his place was not a frequent one. It's a dangerous game to play for a story that would only scandalize a half-run-down detective. Sure, Houston's life would take a hell of a blow, but it wouldn't accomplish anything to drag his name through the mud, really. Nothing of merit.

It's too dangerous for O'Halloran to play that game. *What was it Sal said? Don't piss in your own garden.*

"No, it's not that," Houston says, "though your concern is touching, Detective. Are you *still* a detective, or did they take your badge?"

"Hey now," Exeter says, sounding a little riled up. "Ease up."

Houston hardly feels any desire to do so, but with effort he reins himself in, wondering where the font of his vitriol sprang up today. It feels good to send out blind punches, to use the convenient target of Halward Exeter as a punching bag.

Exeter looks him up and down, once, and seems to read the whole situation, and Houston's anger returns only briefly before it floods out of him leaving him cooler headed. *No point getting mad at Ex.*

"O'Halloran doesn't have anything," Houston lies.

Exeter stares harder, like he knows better.

"Are you gonna tell your partner you're fooling around?" Exeter says, returning a jab with far more precision than Houston's wild swings.

Houston says nothing, seals his angry response up behind his clenched teeth, and turns away. He doesn't want to have this conversation, sees no need to let it continue any further. Houston approaches the counter abruptly, and books the trip to Los Angeles. He pays by check, knowing it will cut into the rent money later.

"What are you going to find there?" Exeter asks, when Houston turns around.

"Answers," Houston tells him.

Exeter's full eyebrows arch upwards once, contorting themselves into a highwire act of disbelief and confusion. Then, incredibly, he steps around Houston and bellies up to the counter of the ticket agent.

"I'll have what he had," Exeter says.

Houston's nearly empty wallet supports the purchase of a newspaper and a pack of cigarettes. He considers getting a paper-wrapped sandwich from the automat machine, but his stomach turns over and plays dead at the thought of food, and refuses to get back up.

Exeter follows along beside him, the hang-dog expression on his determined face telling Houston some volume about the man that he doesn't want to know. The police detective has something to say, some inner turmoil to get off his chest and Houston can hardly escape his own melancholy. He doesn't want to share it with his enemy.

On the train, Exeter shares Houston's compartment, stubbornly refusing to give up the chase, even when Houston puts up the wall of newspaper between them. *If he gets off now, he can still get reimbursement for his ticket*, Houston thinks. Exeter doesn't. He waits, arms folded over his barrel-chest where Houston knows there must be a scar from the shootout on the boat, until the train starts moving.

This efficiently traps Houston and Exeter together.

"Well?" Exeter says, once the steward has come past to check their tickets and give them an arrival time.

Houston debates trying to weasel out of talking about it, to avoid the whole situation by playing coy. Exeter is like a hound with a bone, now, more tenacious than O'Halloran himself was.

"What were *you* doing there, that day?" Houston asks Exeter instead. "Or did he ask for your slice of the Winsome case too?"

"He reeled me in on something else," Exeter admits. "But he did ask me about that night on the boat, yes. About what Punch and Judy said to each other while they were shooting the place up. How's your arm, by the way?"

Houston displays the lack of a cast on his hand, the free way his elbow bends. There's a lingering weakness in the elbow and bicep that he doesn't like and an ugly scar that ripples down over his shoulder and joins with the scar on his inner arm, above the elbow, where it had torn the bicep and broken bone. Thinking about it makes it ache.

"You do physical therapy?" Exeter asks. "I had to. Departmental policy."

Houston shakes his head, looking away. The arm is recovering, that is enough. The thought of spending time churning iron in a gym, smelling sweat and watching the vanity of younger men who thought that strength came from muscles, is enough to set Houston's teeth on edge. Muscles didn't save anybody in the trenches, didn't give anyone an advantage over bombs or Maschinengeweher.

"It was hell," Exeter continues, seeming to echo Houston's thoughts as he turns his impassive eyes from the window to watch Houston. "I got up every day at five a.m. and dragged myself to the hospital where this old battle-axe barked exercises at me until I was ready to drop. If I ever hear the word 'sit up' again, I may snap."

Houston focuses fully on Exeter, wondering again what the detective is doing here.

"Don't you have work to do?" Houston asks, curious in spite of himself.

"It's Saturday," Exeter reminds.

"You're a homicide detective," Houston retorts.

Exeter's jaw tightens, his eyes going dark and deep. This time he turns away, looking back out the window of the train at the passing city—the dark sooty clouds rising out of the dirty snow. The sky is pale and grey, in the way that doesn't promise a fresh blanket of covering snow. It's the sort of day where the sun rolls over and goes back to sleep, pulling the thick down comforter of clouds up over its head and leaving the world below wishing they had the liberty to do the same.

"These days I mostly work the homicide *desk*," Exeter says.

Houston hears this news and understands it, but while other men might have had some sympathy, he can't quite connect how this all relates. What's it supposed to mean that Exeter is here, following him?

"They don't need a desk jockey on a Saturday?" Houston asks, instead of the direct question.

"Will you quit with the tough-guy asshole shtick?" Exeter demands. "Christ, I'd hardly recognize you, these days."

"We never were close enough that you actually knew me, Ex."

"Guess not," Exeter says. "But you owe me an explanation at least. You're the one that kept putting me on all those hinky trails into wonderland. 'Cause of you, I ain't got many friends in the department, these days."

"That's not my fault. You're the one cracking wise at the cop bars and then turning up at the Sappho. What'd you do on raid nights, Ex? You apologize before you cracked some heads?"

"Jesus, Mars."

"They like a thief in the police, but not a homosexual, huh?" Houston hisses, unable to stop the pursuit of his anger; it's like one of those small, angry dogs chasing a car—snapping at the tires like a prey animal at peril of life and limb because of some old haywire wolf instinct that has no other outlet in the modern world.

Exeter sits back, arms crossed over his chest in a defensive position.

"I did my job on that case, Mars," Exeter says, in the level tone of a man who has told himself the same thing for years. "And I did my job on that damn Edward Phillips case you set me on, and that frozen actor that's got you so worked up. So for all your yapping about that case you say I stole five years ago, I surely and truly wish to God I had never taken the ones you *handed* to me, because look where it's gotten me."

Houston's fury begins to fade—a little, weighed down under the foundation of common decency that's the structure on which the core of himself is built. His responsibility is for drawing attention to Exeter's secrets, but he won't take any for the secrets themselves. He starts to take a breath to respond, and Exeter cuts him off.

"Will you shut up for ten seconds, you righteous prick?" Exeter snaps. "I'm here because your damn partner is worried about you."

"Sal?" Houston asks, surprised.

"No, the little green leprechaun you work cases with. Do you have another partner?"

Houston closes his mouth, meeting Exeter's gaze and waiting for explanation.

"Costanzo contacted me. Said you've been behaving strangely and you didn't come into the office yesterday," Exter elucidates. "He was worried, but he wouldn't say it. Wanted to know if we'd crossed paths on this thing you're working on, and I'm not supposed to be working on."

Houston thinks of the short meeting outside O'Halloran's place, before the guilt at what he did there rises up.

"What'd you tell him?" he asks, pushing his anxious feelings away.

Exeter gives Houston a measuring look, a long slow drag of his ponderous gaze over Houston's features that suggests he knows enough about Houston and Sal to make an educated guess as to why the answer to this question is significant.

"I told him I'd keep an eye out," Exeter says. "A fact for which you might consider owing me a favor."

"I'll consider it. And by keeping an eye out, you meant you'd follow me like a shadow?"

"I didn't at the time. But never interrupt an enemy when he's making a mistake." As if he were delivering all the wisdom of the pharaohs, Exeter continues, "Follow him while he's doing it and laugh."

In spite of himself, Houston cracks a grim smile. *Maybe it is a mistake, chasing this thing across the country and into the west, but it's my mistake to make. If Exeter wants to follow me—even if it's only to laugh—let him.*

"Alright," Houston says, relenting. "If you're so inclined. But I'm not sharing a sleeping car with you."

The countryside rolls by outside the window, from city to the sleepy and untouched areas of the Illinois wasteland beyond the clean-cut of the train tracks, lancing away over the snowy fields. It could be any of a hundred landscapes Houston saw in the war, save for the absence of trenches.

Beyond the city, the houses that cluster close to the tracks are empty, leaning, showing signs of age. The ghost of the former boom now haunting the chilly countryside. Houston watches the world that spring should be transforming with dispassionate eyes, certain the world is unready for so hopeless a season.

The weather would become more forgiving for the homeless bodies scattered over the ground, putting fewer beneath it until the pendulum of seasons swung forward again, bringing summer on with all it's soupy humidity, ready to put the fire under the cookpot of humanity left without any finances for shelter.

For a time, they're both quiet. Houston's tired mind turns around on the new information before it eases over into rest. Exeter picks up the *Tribune* forgotten at Houston's side and runs his eyes over it without lingering too long on any one article.

If O'Halloran's working on a doozy about the Winsome case, it hasn't hit yet. Houston wonders again about Exeter's presence at the reporter's house.

"Do you think they'll find him guilty?" Houston asks.

"Depends," Exeter says. "He'll be guilty of killing Edgar, and with his wife and all..."

It's a sympathetic picture to any jury.

"The rest," Exeter shrugs. "If his lawyer's any good, he'll make sure the jury is sympathetic to the wrong voice. Maybe they won't feel it's such a crime to kill a guy like Edward Phillips or Charles Winsome. Might lead to a hung jury."

Implicit in the statement is that these sorts of upstanding, jury-of-your-peers citizens wouldn't mind too much if it were Houston or Exeter's body up there on the altar of evidence.

"Winsome's on the state's dime, though," Exeter continues. "So who knows how that plays out. You were at the hearing?"

Houston shakes his head. "I wasn't called. I've got a deposition for the trial."

Exeter makes a scolding cluck with his tongue. "I'll pretend I didn't hear that."

"You spoke to O'Halloran, too."

"I read him the cease-and-desist riot act. That crackpot reporter's been calling everybody. The wife, the DA, trying to get an interview with Winsome himself. *You*, apparently."

"We hardly talked about it," Houston says, realizing it's the truth.

Exeter gives Houston a strange look, vaguely uncertain. It's one of those moments where Houston realizes he's set himself up for a question he doesn't want to answer.

"He interviewed Lucas a couple of years ago," Houston says, not sure why it seems so important to correct Exeter's assumption about what he was doing with the reporter when it was a sound one. It's almost impossible to fool a detective with a good hunch. "I wanted to know if he'd learned anything that wasn't in the paper."

"About you?" Exeter prompts.

"Not everything's about hiding your sins, Ex. Lucas vanished in 1926, then two years ago he came back around to Chicago and I didn't even know he was here."

"Maybe he didn't want you to," Exeter says, smiling. The jab lands off-center, hitting the truth like a lance.

"He didn't. Something happened to him in Los Angeles, bad enough that he couldn't really brag about his success. Whatever it was, it put him on the path to his end, Ex. I can't accept that his death was an accident when I know what I know, and I can't let it go without learning the rest, either."

"You can't stop it. It's already over."

The logic is sound, but there's a churning anger in Houston's gut. A foreign desire for violent revenge lodged in his intestines like a parasite, twisting his guts up into a war against themselves. "I can stop it from happening to someone else."

Exeter sits back in the upholstered seat of the train car, crossing his arms over his chest.

"The law won't do it," Houston continues, compelled by Exeter's silent gaze and heavy judgment to go on.

"They'll get what's coming to them," Exeter soothes. "But are you sure you want to transform who you are enough to be the one to give it to them?"

It's a point that lodges in Houston's body like a knife. He examines himself, just a little—his situation, the things that have been surrounding him since he's started looking into this. How little anything else in his life but *knowing* seems to matter.

"I just want to know the answers," Houston admits. "I want to look whoever did it in the eyes myself and decide if I should ruin them."

Beyond the terminator line of winter, the train from the small state-run line out of Chicago lets out onto the Southern Pacific by way of Ogden, Utah. California beckons with grass-turned-gold, not so much as a slushpile to be seen in the early spring sunlight. The 22nd comes and goes as Houston shares company —usually silent—with Exeter.

After a time, the quiet and patience starts to gnaw at his resolve. At their last stop, Exeter purchased a dime-novel western with men and horses on the cover, recalling an age before the war with such glory and wistfulness that Houston almost feels drawn into the idea himself.

The pages fold and turn slowly in his big hands, and he gives no outward sign of interest in Houston. Houston tries to think ahead, to plan out any of a dozen scenarios for what he'll do when they reach the city.

By now, Houston's accepted his presence through sheer determination. If Exeter hasn't peeled off of him, as the sun sets on Sunday evening and carries Exeter over into the irrevocable choice to skip work the next day, he isn't going to. It's more dedication than Houston expects—he thought maybe at the edge of Illinois that Exeter would have washed his hands of this.

Finally, Exeter folds the book closed and looks up at Houston. "Do you know what we're going to do when we get there?"

"We?"

"I'm here aren't I? You really want to face these guys alone?"

"I have an address," Houston sighs.

"From two years ago?"

"I know a few names, too. But I have this gut feeling that I'm going to find something at the address. I have... there's another case, too. A producer."

California is gold and glistening, the rolling fields like the picture on Exeter's book cover. In San Francisco, the train pauses to refuel, to restock itself, to disgorge its passengers into the heart of what was once gold-rush territory. Now all evidence of a boom town gone bust.

There's still the rush and bustle along the hilly, narrow streets. Houston peers out from the train-car window and then feels the itch in his bones to get out. They have about three hours—enough time to find food, if any place here can feed Houston and leave him enough for the transit fares in Los Angeles.

"People must have heart attacks out here all the time," Exeter observes, looking down the hill that South Pacific Station is perched on and toward Mission Bay. The stark black lines of a bridge cut across it, gleaming metal with lines of cars nose-to-end and moving over the artery as slowly as the pulsing blood of a man asleep.

"You could wait here," Houston offers.

"I'm hungry too, you louse," Exeter says. "I practically haven't eaten since we started on this cockamaimie trip because I didn't want to let you out of my sight."

"Am I that much of an eyefull, Ex?"

"An *eyesore*, maybe. No, I don't trust you not to disappear."

Exeter shouldn't, but Houston makes no effort to leave him behind as they head along King St. and he scans the street for signs of a promising lunch-counter—even an automat.

"Come on, there's a deli this way," Exeter says at last, when he there's no sign of purpose in Houston's searching. Exeter turns down a side-street that seems barely wide enough for pedestrians, leading between the tall, strange buildings fit over the hill like an uneven crown descending the side of it. The alley twists back uphill and away from the train station, letting them out on a little street that allows cars only one way.

"You've been to San Francisco before?" Houston asks, as Exeter chugs his way through the morning traffic.

"You," Exeter pants, "haven't?"

They stop at the top of the hill, and Exeter catches his breath before opening the door into the delicatessen, an affair with German and English copies of the menu on the front of the door along with prices written out. As the door closes behind him, Houston can see the piece of paper on the back with a matching list in Yiddish Hebrew, and inside the sweet-cheese and smoked-ham scented store, Houston would guess it's the predominant language being spoken.

Several tables line the front window, and along the wall to the far side, leaving an open walkway across the floor to the counter where smoked ham hocks are hung up behind the proprietor. He is a thin, nervous looking man who does not sport the beard and curls, nor the shtreimel of the Hassidic Jew. Instead, he has the clean shaven face and well-brushed black, wavy hair of one well and truly Americanized.

The back of his head is covered from the eyes of God with a crocheted yarmulke, perched cautiously there as if on the very centerpoint between the man's faith and acceptance of the gaps in the American tolerance for anything different.

"What will you gentlemen have?" the proprietor asks, with the well faded warmth of a German accent, as he works his hands clean on an immaculate rag.

Exeter places his order in Yiddish, which sounds rusty and tarnished in his rough voice, but seems to get the point across, and sparks a conversation that leaves Houston standing lost on foreign soil. The points he can follow are gestures, one of which indicates him, leaving him tucking his hands into his pockets a bit like a guilty schoolboy.

In the end, Exeter hands Houston a pastrami-on-rye with the best stone-ground mustard he's ever had, and takes a bowl of cold Kasha for himself even though the morning is wearing on. They sit out back in the tiny courtyard between buildings, fenced in on all sides by the strange, slanted-seeming houses.

"Alright," Houston says. "I give up. I wouldn't have placed you as-"

"I'm not," Exeter says. "My mother was, over from Poland in the last century."

"I thought that passed through the mother."

"Not when your father was the one I had."

Houston can see the description of a tyrant in Exeter's behavior, then. How the man must have stood over his son's life and held the reins, whipping all the way. It's the image of a cowboy that isn't romanticized, the hard-drinking and violent man who exercised what control he could muster over the lives of those around him when he found his cowboy age dying in its boots around him. The age of the horse and the gold rush have passed, rendering such men useless edifices of the past, powerless except over their kin.

"Alright," Houston says, avoiding the deep dive off the edge of the cliff he's standing on. "So, you know your way around San Francisco, how about you tell me about that?"

"Nothing to tell," Exeter says. "I spent the first fifteen years of my life here. Then all the sun got to me."

Houston sinks his teeth into his sandwich and chews, trying not to become too involved in Exeter. There's enough here to reach out and wrap his hands around it, to begin to understand someone he's never had the desire to understand while all of the bare parts of him are surfacing and glinting in the sun.

"We spent the summers in Los Angeles," Exeter continues, stirring his cereal with a sluggish spoon. "Never made much sense to me, going south when it was hotter, but that was where we went. I know my way around the city, if you've got wet feet down there, too."

"We were on the east coast," Houston says. "Things were different before the war. Nice Yankees didn't go west."

Exeter snorts. "So what's your excuse?"

Houston doesn't argue against the jab he set himself up for, giving Exeter the coup as his own to count.

"Anyway, thanks," Houston says, chewing his sandwich. He makes it through half before he sets the other half down—feeling little interest in eating. There's been a heavy weight in his middle since he started the journey, taking up space and leaving him full without even the thought of food to distract him. He wraps the uneaten portion in the wax paper from the plate bottom—a red and white checker pattern—and tucks it into his pocket. He doesn't want to eat it, but can't abide throwing it away.

"You wanna know what I think?" Exeter puts in, then, as if Houston has invited him.

Houston looks up, waiting, sitting back in his chair in the warm air that's trapped in the funnel of crooked buildings here, not sure if he really does want to know.

"You oughta let this whole thing lie," Exeter says. "It's years past and bigger than you."

"Ex," Houston says, smiling a little, unable to help his grin. "The building's way bigger than the wrecking ball."

"So Confucious says," Exeter agrees begrudgingly. He finishes his bowl of cereal, and Houston carries their dishes back inside and thanks the man behind the counter for his excellent meal.

The walk back up to the train station is every bit as punishing as expected, with Exeter's train-stack chugging alongside Houston. He thinks about what he knows now, about what he faces in the future, far south in California.

"Okay, so," Exeter says, huffing, as they reach the summit of the hill. "How about you, wise guy?"

"How about me, what?" Houston pauses to light a cigarette as they catch their breath. By now the pack he bought Sunday is less than half full.

"You said you were from back east," Exeter reminds, as if patiently leading a child through an exercise in logic. "Where, exactly? Are you a Chicago boy?"

"I was never a boy," Houston says, digging in his pocket for his ticket. A strange pain flares up in his shoulder, spreading downward, as he pats the checkbook pocket for the crinkling stub of punched paper. A weakness like a pinched nerve that startles him, and Houston drops the arm to his side, alternating to his other hand.

"Just sprang up out of your mama's vegetable patch, huh?" Exeter asks. "No wonder you got funny ideas about sex."

"Alright, alright, I get it."

The compartment they return to has been cleaned, and Houston measures the space with his eyes, as if seeing it for the first time. It looks dingy and old, a relic from another era. *How much longer will Trains survive in this world of airplanes and easy travel?* He wonders if he can expect to see the demise of many things over the span of his life.

"I'm from Connecticut," he says. "Nowhere special in it, exactly. I was grown when I left, and I headed west."

"Gold? Cowboys?" Exeter lowers himself heavily and with great relish to the seat on the other side of the cabin, watching Houston with satisfaction—as if getting him talking about the past is something he could tally up in his book of small victories.

"Just away from where I was. Like you did."

"And the war? I don't remember much from your tour at the academy, but I remember you were a veteran."

"Medical," Houston corrects. "I served as a surgeon's assistant for a while, that's all. I'd started school for it in Michigan."

"How 'bout that," Exeter says with wonder. "How come you came back to be a cop and not a doctor? It'd suit you better to fix people up rather than tear 'em down."

"For that opinion, I guess I should thank you, but I lost the stomach for it. I never really liked it to begin with. Did you serve?"

"Over there? Yeah," Exeter admits. "A short term. I took two in the leg, and for a while they thought they were going to have to saw it off."

He pauses, reaching down, pulling up the leg of his grey suit so that the mud-stained cuff lifts past his ankle, displaying two closely-spaced and well healed star-marks in the calf. Bullet wounds. Houston would bet the make and caliber matched the German Luger, but he's seen a lot of such scars.

"They shipped me back, and by the time I finished in the hospital, the whole thing was over," Exeter says. "I went back to the police force."

"Suits you."

"Hey now, I thought we were being nice."

Houston turns his gaze to look out the window, and thinks for the first time of his family; of the stack of unopened cards sitting in a hat box in his closet. He wonders why they still write, why they keep up the facade of even having a son anymore. The war provided them with an ample and identifiable excuse to claim Houston's loss. The cards that come are all in his mother's handwriting, and he doesn't know what the interiors say, but he bets they're as bland and sterile as the last phone conversation he had with her, when he got back from the war, when he told her he wasn't going to finish medical school. The whole time he was on the phone, the line from the earpiece to the phone's base reminded him of the miles and miles of wire that boys had crawled beneath razor-wire to lay, dragging it out for miles behind their bodies before a sapper came and cut it, or before they found a bomb and their lines were suddenly cut short.

He retreats back away from the conversation, leaning his chin against the palm of his hand, and thinks about how he's dragged himself through all the mud of his life since he met Lucas, and now here, *still,* he's trying to lay out enough line along his tedious path to connect them together again, Point A to Point B, to hear that one last transmission that's trapped in the wire.

6.

By the time they make it to Los Angeles, Houston can feel the weight of his sleeplessness on his shoulders, can feel the way his body is sluggish and refusing to move forward without wading through a morass of sticky resistance.

"Tell me you got a hotel before we go tilting at this windmill," Exeter says, practically stumbling along. He closed his eyes on the last leg of the journey, his breath evening out and his silence matching Houston's, but Houston only watched the day fold itself down into night along the length of the California coast, the sun setting behind the mountains. The cliffs suddenly dropped away and revealed the Pacific Ocean, shining and green and choppy with the evening waves as it mirrored the yellows and reds of the sunset.

"You think they'll all be booked up?" Houston asks, looking around at the empty streets surrounding the train station. A dozen young palm trees, transplants from somewhere far more exotic than the ass-end of America, seem to have sprung up alongside the streets, each shorter than the buildings on either side of them. Their youth, and the brown, shaggy leaves hanging from beneath their more hopeful canopies seems to say a lot about the state of the city.

"No," Exeter admits. "Come on, we'll head up Broadway. Wish I'd brought a change of clothes."

Houston agrees, following Exeter like a faithful hound deeper into the city. It smells more oceanic than San Francisco, with a deep fish-stink pouring up from its gutters as the city cools and belches steam from the hot drainage system beneath. The evening is already turning cold, a breeze in off the coast making Houston turn up his collar, when earlier in the day he'd have gone down to his shirt sleeves. He has never understood these desert dwellers, nor the driving need to transform—at least to the eye—a wasteland into an oasis.

As if by sheer determination and Hollywood magic they can transform it into something more hospitable, making a silk purse from this sow's ear. Or at least drive up the property values on land where very little could grow or thrive.

If so, the joke is on them—instead of seeing a lush and verdant paradise, Houston sees a paper bag with the bottom soaked but the sides crisp, ready for the whole load of bullshit inside of it to drop out at any second.

The spaces beneath bridges are filled with ramshackle shelters, and men and women sit on street corners in despondent and paralyzed hope, tiny cups set out with words like 'please' written on them in grease pencil or lipstick.

Exeter leads them to a hotel alongside one of the streets lit with the electric light poles installed between the anemic palm trees. It's a big, square building that speaks of economy. The bottom story painted a brighter color, though now the paint is faded. It has big windows there, as if there had once been storefronts, but two of these are empty and the third is only a newsshop and bookstore, with the shelves full of carefully spaced product spread out to look full.

"Hell," Houston says, patting his pocket for his checkbook. "This isn't the town they tell us it should be in the movies."

"Nowhere's like it seems in the movies," Exeter agrees. "With a last name like 'Mars' you should know that."

"Maybe things used to be."

"Ain't nothing like it used to be, either. Go inside, I'm freezing my ass off."

Inside, Houston writes a check to the clerk who looks down-right nervous about taking it, and demands twenty dollars in cash as a deposit on two seven dollar hotel rooms. Houston wonders if the man wants to check his teeth, too, as he shows his investigator's license for identification.

"I don't have that in cash," Houston starts to fold his check back into his hand. His wallet has a total of seventeen bucks in ones and fives. "There another place that doesn't have such a steep deposit?"

"I got it," Exeter grumbles, fishing out his wallet to produce the required amount. "Don't think you won't owe me, Mars."

"Sorry," the desk clerk says, without a hint of apology. "It's the times these days. More bad checks than good. I'll phone your bank in the morning and you can have your deposit back."

Houston steps out of the way to let Exeter book, and they take adjoining rooms, without Houston bothering to protest. He doesn't want to say anything more than he has to in front of the weasel-faced clerk, and he takes his key and his meager stack of bath towels without further comment.

"There's no bellboy this late," the clerk says, his accent lacka-daisical in comparison to the rapid-patter of the two men from Chicago. "Do you have any luggage you'd like me to bring up?"

Houston trades a glance with Exeter and shrugs. "No thanks, Charley, I think we can manage."

They take the stairs, passing two floors before they come out into the dimly lit hallways; old fleur-de-lis wallpaper is more or less clean and more or less sticking to the walls of their home for the night, cream on blue in a way that reminds Houston of his mother's old Wedgwood table service. Along the tall base-boards, a layer of grime has accumulated, a darkening of the once-brilliant white paint that cries out to be revisited with a brush and careful attention.

"Well," Houston observes. "It ain't the Ritz."

"I get the impression that between the two of us, we can't afford the Ritz," Exeter says. "Shut up and go take a shower and get some sleep. I'm barely upright and I'm betting you've been sleeping like a dog that likes to chase cars."

Houston takes the advice, admitting himself into a square, adequately sized room. The carpet is thin, the floor itself shifting a little in a resigned and tired fashion underfoot as he peers into the bathroom, as he investigates every drawer and cabinet in some old, wondering habit. He finds soap and shampoo, and in the dresser there's a King James bible placed there for his education. He closes the drawer again and leaves it that way, knowing that the bible has very little to say to him aside from "stay away."

Houston hangs his suit on the hook in the closet, brushing it down to remove the worst of the clinging grime before he heads into the bathroom in his underwear. He drops it and his socks in the hotel sink, filling the basin with hot tap water and white soap. He gives the offensive garments a scrub, working the material methodically between his hands and the bar until the worst of the sweat is out, then rinses both until the grey water runs clear. He drains the sink, his mind a distant blank that fails to fully register the melancholy tragedy of washing his underwear in a hotel bathroom.

He wrings the garments out, and hangs them up over the heater coil, kicking the gas on with the valve to a low roil. Then he steps into the shower and washes away the grime of travel and the exhaustion of his thoughts. The water is hot, and scrubbing the rough white cloth over his skin leaves Houston almost more energized, revitalizes him briefly as he washes his hair, rinses his mouth, and then turns off the tap.

The clock on the nightstand reads after midnight when he lowers himself to the bed, bare as the day he was born. The small, old gas-lamp fixture sheds a tired, pale yellow circle of light into the room as he sits back against the headboard and thinks a little on how he's come to be in this place. His mind feels too keyed up and alert to sleep while his body feels leaden and cries out for rest. Houston can't will his thoughts to go still.

Reaching for the nightstand, he pulls open the drawer with a paper-dry sounding slide, revealing the bible within—a plain, red, hard cover. He flips it open, the thin, onion-skin pages wafting up a disused smell, parchment and dust and days at church that Houston hasn't thought about in a long time.

He flips through, eyes on the pages without really registering. Then, in a curling hand, a message on one of the blank pages in the back. *A friend loves at all times, and a brother is born for a time of adversity.* Houston runs his eyes over the bible verse, copied out for posterity, and then puts the book away, reaching up to turn off the light.

The bed sheets are scratchy and starch-hardened against his bare skin, and for a moment, he's deeply aware of the adjoining door between his room and Exeter's, of the implication of trust there.

It's a world in which he cannot ever expect to know the future, that's for sure.

7.

With the room lights out, he can see the light of the city beyond the filmy curtains, and feel the scratch of the blanket against his side as he bunches the deflated hotel pillow under his head and his mind begins the motions required for sleep, even though he's exhausted. It's akin to a dog turning around three times before laying down.

Then consciousness fades back from him instead of the sharp drop off of sleep, and time spins away, leaving Houston uncertain as to whether he's slept at all when he becomes aware of the window lightening. He feels rested, alert, anxious. There's a low twisting in his belly that comes with the awareness that today he'll have at least one more answer.

He gets up, swinging his bare legs over the side of the bed, and feels the cold air roll against his skin as all of his trapped body heat evaporates from beneath the covers, driving a sudden shiver through him.

Houston calls down for room-service, and then recovers his stiff, dry underwear from where it hangs. There's still some residual heat from the heater below them, and Houston pulls them on quickly, and splashes water on his unshaven face in the sink. He can feel the tiny, coarse hairs getting longer, and his reflection looks dark-eyed in the mirror, a liquid gleam in the depths of them that seems sleepless and eternal.

Houston looks away, gathers his suit, and taps on the adjoining door into Exeter's room to wake him.

"Go to hell," Exeter calls back. "It's two hours earlier in California, go back to bed."

"There's coffee coming."

"I'll drink it cold, goddamnit," Exeter snaps, and Houston can hear the angry shuffle of his heavy body on the bed, the way the headboard taps the wall behind it as he rolls over, probably to stuff a pillow over his head.

Houston doesn't knock again, glancing up at the clock to find it reads just 6:00—an earlier time than his usual wakeup, but he has little desire to return to bed. He pulls on his pants and his shirt sleeves over his boxers and undershirt. When the tired looking bellboy shows up with his food, he fishes some change out of the dwindling supply of coins in his pocket.

He sits down with the newspaper, and is startled by the date. *March 26th*—almost the end of the month. Where had it gone? Within a week, it will be April. Some of it was travel, some of it the introspection and agony required to make the leap.

It hardly matters.

There are two newspapers on the tray, one the *Chicago Tribune*; Houston guesses the desk man figured his origin from the bank address on his check. Smart man, attentive to detail. He unfolds the paper cautiously, like a man pulling a venomous snake out of its basket.

The front page is a cascade of information about the Winsome case, a long side-column scrolling down the left-hand side of the paper from top to bottom. Houston skims it over, but he sees the byline isn't O'Halloran's. Curiously, he checks over the whole front page, all lead up to the jury trial's date being set in Cook County. There's no sign of O'Halloran's bombshell. Houston finds this curious, and he considers what it means as he slowly imbibes his cup of coffee before the city lights beyond the windows start to turn off.

Houston pulls back the thin curtain at last, leaving the *Tribune* behind. A quick glance at the L.A. rag reveals that the DOJ is running a big crackdown sting in the city, busting up enough operations to unsettle the Mob. Houston doesn't read any further. L.A. is just like every other big city right now, swamped with problems created by prohibition and the stock market crash. Underneath that bright warning light of trouble, the homeless and desperate are drawn into the spaces between buildings to starve quietly with their cups out.

There are already cars moving in the city, Houston can see their headlights navigating the narrow maze of streets—but here the city spreads out flat, a quiet sister to San Francisco far to the north, with its slanting lines. There are already taller skyscrapers beginning to form—or perhaps the efforts are abandoned; the skeletons of steel and concrete only partially formed against the purpling sky. Houston finishes his first cup of coffee, and fills the second before Exeter's knock proceeds him into the room.

"You couldn't let a guy sleep," he grouches, reaching up to blind Houston by turning on the gas lamp, lighting it with a match from a book in his pocket. He's half dressed, his normally neat short hair raised into a cowlick in back.

"Coffee's still hot," Houston offers, indicating the carafe on the service.

"Is that all you're having for breakfast?" Exeter wonders, looking over the wheeled tray. The rest of the standard fare is beneath a plain metal cover, a holdover from a time when the hotel had attracted more clientele than two detectives of various grades. There's sausage—cheaper than bacon—and a heap of eggs, with two slices of toast to one side.

"If you want it, take it," Houston says.

Exeter sits down on the edge of Houston's bed and wheels the tray closer to himself, seasoning the cooling eggs with salt and hot sauce in a way that makes Houston's stomach turn over, before he helps himself to the food. Houston feels distant and ethereal when he thinks about what's gone into his body over the last few days. Coffee, mostly. Half a sandwich Tuesday. He's still not hungry, but he takes a piece of toast to settle his stomach.

"I have an address," Houston says. "Do you know your way around town enough to get us there, or should I call the desk and ask for a map?"

"Where is it?"

"North Hollywood, I think," Houston says. From the inner pocket of his suit coat, he produces the slip of paper with O'Halloran's writing on it.

Exeter looks it over without making any move to take it, raking his eyes over it as he hangs over the plate of food like a vulture over a carcass. His gaze is accusatory. "Dan O'Halloran gave you that."

"I thought that was pretty clear," Houston puts the paper away again.

"Well, I know where that is. That whole area is the wannabes of Hollywood," Exeter says, in clear displeasure. "Tenants go in and out of there like roaches wandering through your kitchen."

"Maybe not this one."

"Yeah, okay." Exeter goes back to chewing. "I can get us there. Didn't you say there was a sister in New York?"

"They weren't in contact."

"Maybe not when you knew him, but if he was desperate for money, he might have got back in touch."

Houston wants to deny this. No matter how desperate he's gotten over the course of his time away from home, he's never once reached back, never once opened or answered a letter, though he kept them just the same.

He shakes his head, but resists the urge to explain his hunch.

"I'll get there when I get there," Houston says. "Whatever she knows, I still need to follow the trail here."

Exeter, poking his tongue into his cheek to chase some bit of breakfast, makes a conciliatory motion with his eyebrows and then shoves the tray away. "You wanna go bust heads on this at six am?"

Houston supposes not.

"Come on," Exeter says, getting up. "I gotta make a phone call, then let's walk it out. Take some of the edge off before you hit this thing with more force than is maybe wise."

Houston can hear the sullen, heavy footsteps as Exeter heads downstairs for the phone at the desk, carrying his coffee cup with him.

Houston spends a few minutes getting his shoes on, watching the sky grow lighter outside the window, reds and yellows reaching out to touch the corners of the sprawling city. He pushes the emptied tray out into the hall, as Exeter returns with his emptied cup. Ex leaves it on the tray when he sees Houston is ready.

"You get through?" Houston asks idly. "Early to call back home."

"I left a message."

The tired looking clerk glowers suspiciously at them as they head out into the early light, and Houston wonders how many security deposits it would take to make him feel more inclined to the hospitality that is his job.

"Alright, let's get some of the town underfoot," Exeter suggests, as they step out onto the sidewalk. It's still cool, but nothing like the cold of Chicago, and the day promises to warm up quickly. "They cut this jagged hole in the ground last year and I hear they opened a theater there in January."

"Sure," Houston says. He remembers reading about the Grauman's Chinese Theatre in the *Tribune*, hearing a fluff piece on the evening news. "There was a whole to-do, all that money into something so frivolous as a movie house."

"Gotta do something with what you've got before it goes away," Exeter says. He led them onto a main thoroughfare, already busy with pedestrian and car traffic. Houston can see, erected in the hills beyond the limits of the city, a massive sign with white lettering. *Hollywoodland.*

"What's that about," he asks, taken aback by the gaudy nature of the thing, like printing your name across God's landscape.

"There's a housing development back there," Exeter says, his tone bland with displeasure. "In fact, the place we're headed is up there, hidden away before Mulholland Drive picks up and the real stars appear."

"What do you mean real stars?" Houston asks as Exeter leads the way up past the massive facade of the new theater. They turn on Vine up toward the hills beyond, following the street toward where the pavement ends and begins a looping, dirt-road ascent up into the hilly California countryside.

"You'll see," Exeter says. "We can hope your lead's an early riser. Should be nearly nine by the time we get up there."

They walk for a long time in silence, leaving puffs of dust as they walk along the shoulder of the road. The occasional bus rattles by tempting fate and sending up plumes of the dry, fine dirt that covers the packed road surface. Eventually they can step away from the edge and back onto a paved street, the concrete new under all the brown dust from the trail.

"Now I know where they get all those ideas for cars going over cliffs in the movies," Houston remarks, patting dust off his pants. Ahead, he can see massive, palatial homes—castles built of stone and stucco, with tile roofs or turrets. Houston gives a low whistle, thinking about Sal's poem. "Safe upon the solid rock, the ugly houses stand…"

"Yeah, yeah, *palace on the sand*," Exeter waves Houston off from his droll quotation. "That's what I meant by real stars. We're not going there.

Houston hesitates anyway, looking over the well-fortified bastions of the very rich and famous, and wonders how long they'll stay there in this great depression. He wonders how many of those very same boom homes, once touted as prestigious havens in a community that would thrive for decades, are even now standing empty.

"Must be nice," Houston says, "being a star."

"Must be why everybody wants to be one," Exeter agrees. "Not a lot of folks make it. It's still tough to get in. Boys and girls get hopeful, then hit that glass ceiling. You have to have the looks, the charm, the willingness to suck—"

"Stop," Houston says through grit teeth.

Exeter glances at him, closing his mouth, as if uncertain why Houston would be sensitive. Then he jams his hands in his pockets, and reaches up to tip his hat down. Houston thinks it gives the impression of someone too proud to apologize when they realize they've touched a nerve.

The Hollywood Stay-A-While is a strange, square building with boxy porches hung off the sides of it, recesses beneath those that then jut out into offset porches of their own. It's a blocky jumble of a building, like a child's forgotten tower of blocks, occasionally interrupted by a wandering jew vine hanging out of a pot, or a caged canary fluttering around in the morning's growing warmth and singing out small, hopeful sounds to the world beyond the black iron bars.

Houston counts numbers on the doors, and Exeter lingers behind. Silent. Waiting. When Houston finds the apartment he's seeking, it's on the ground floor, identical to the other units. The porch is barren of anything but a scratched glass table, a bare iron chair, and an overflowing ashtray. He taps on the door with his knuckles, making the sound faint and polite rather than the heavy-handed knock he uses to announce his presence as a detective.

No one answers. Houston gives it a moment, and then taps again. A voice raises inside, calling out in a groggy tone something that Houston can't quite make out, so he steps back and waits. If no one answers soon, he'll hit the door with a little more force.

Finally, the door cracks open and a bloodshot eye peers out, the rest of the person hidden behind the barrier of a chain and the barely opened door. The man is thin, with the dark-circled and yet flame-bright eyes of an addict. The one cheekbone Houston can see is sharply defined over a drawn face, and the hair is lank with inattention.

"Who are you?" the man asks.

"I'm looking for a man named Lucas Harcourt," Houston says, "Are you his roommate?"

"He ain't around," the man says, suddenly angry. "And if you find him, tell him he skipped out on rent."

It's the answer Houston needs. "You are his roommate."

"Me and half the block," the man sneers. "But I'm the one that *pays* to be here."

"Lucas is dead," Houston says flatly, looking for signs of a surprised reaction.

"Well then I guess you know where to find him."

The junkie begins to swing the door closed again, closing the divide of only inches, and Houston jams the toe of his shoe into the frame, keeping it open.

"I was hoping you could answer some questions for me," he says, as the man struggles to close the door. Houston keeps his foot angled so the sole of his shoe takes the brunt of the force from the door and not his vulnerable toes.

"Hell no, man," the junkie says. "Get lost."

"Step back from the door," Houston warns, his tone sounding strange even to his own ears. He's aware that Exeter is coming up behind him, approaching from the sidewalk.

"What—" the junkie starts to ask.

Houston throws his shoulder into the door, slamming himself against it hard enough to yank the screws of the chain plate free of the door jam, swinging the door open and inward with a tremendous force. The sudden bright pain in Houston's injured shoulder feels good; it feels like the first sensation that's made it through to him in a while, waking him up out of his stupor and bringing him alive again.

"Houston, *Jesus*," Exeter says, as Houston shoves his way inside, but he makes no effort to bar his entrance.

"Get out of here! Get out!" the man shouts as he scrambles backwards. Houston spares a brief thought for the neighbors—but a closer look at the man's body reveals all the telltale traits of what his father would have called a "junkman." Houston's first assessment was correct, and a junkie rarely endears himself to his community.

He's the skinny twitching kind, the polar opposite to Sal's languid distance—a cocaine user.

"Sit down," Houston orders, closing the door behind him and Exeter, with only a brief glance at the torn door frame and the no longer secured plate dangling from the chain—short screws, a common fault of new housing.

The junkie complies, sitting sullenly on the only available furniture—a battered couch along the wall adjacent to the door.

The rest of the space is devoid of anything but a few old shipping crates on the floor, a scattering of plates over the inset kitchen countertop on the other side of the door frame. All the signs of a chronic drug user at the end of his rope, with nothing left to sell.

"I don't have any money," the junkie protests, wild-eyed and trembling on the couch. There's a tic at the corner of his mouth, pulling the muscles of his face, tight-loose-tight. Houston realizes he's barely dressed, in only a dingy T-shirt and boxers "Whatever he owes you I had nothing to do with it and I can't pay it."

"We ain't here for money," Exeter puts in, giving Houston a brief, extremely dark look—the sort that suggested they'd talk later, probably at a loud volume. For now, while they're here, Exeter seems to have his back.

"Well—well, you said he was dead," the junkie says, as if unable to comprehend anything that the pair of them could be there for except money. The drug has crossed and recrossed all the wires in his brain until he thinks only in terms of dollars and deals.

Houston leaves Exeter by the door and reaches out, picks up an old crate and dumps a half dozen classified sections from old newspapers out of it over the man's living room floor.

"Hey—" the junkie begins to protest.

Houston slams the crate upside down on the carpet, silencing him, feeling far less tough than he probably looks when his shoulder weakens in the middle of the motion. Anything would look real and solid to this trembling shadow of a man, it looks like a stiff breeze would throw him down clattering like a skeleton. Houston sits on the crate across from the man on the dirty couch and looks him in the eyes.

"I have reason to believe there was a certain type of pressure on Lucas from his employer, a Hollywood producer," Houston explains gruffly, then waits until he's sure that the junkie is focused on him and listening. "I also have reason to believe that these actions led directly to his death. So I need you to tell me when you last saw Lucas, and what was happening to him before he disappeared."

"What?" the man manages, looking back and forth between Houston and Exeter, weighing the carrot against the stick. He seems to see nothing but immovable walls, one in front of him and one between him and the exit.

"Tell me about what was happening before Lucas disappeared." After a moment of staring hard into the junkie's shuddering-leaf eyes, Houston leans back taking a little pity on him. Remembering the overflowing ashtray outside, Houston reaches into the inner pocket of his suit. He offers the first Chesterfield he shakes free of the pack to the bewildered junkie.

"You kicked down my door, now you want to be pals with me?" the man asks, his wavering voice stumbling toward outrage. He reaches for the cigarette anyway.

When he takes it, Houston offers a lit match, his hands steadier than the junkie's. A good quarter-inch of the cigarette sucks in and backward under the red line of cherry, transforming to ash in the first inhalation. It seems to steady the junkie a little.

"I want you to answer my questions," Houston says.

"Who the hell are you, anyway?" the junkie demands.

Houston doesn't answer the question, instead lighting a cigarette for himself then leaning back again to give the junkie space to answer. The man drags a shaking hand through his hair, and puts the cigarette to his thin mouth again, showing a hint of his teeth. Maybe once, he would have been handsome, but his steady diet of deprivation and chemical highs have left him a ragged remain—the sort of thing you find by the side of the road after a major accident—some tatter that belonged to some article of clothing at one point in time. Maybe with a stain you didn't want to look at on it.

"Alright," the junkie gives in to the silent pressure. "Lucas was last here, I guess... before Christmas, I remember. Before that he was in and out all the time. He kept going out, trying to get jobs. He needed the money for—well, for rent, in part."

"How was he paying rent before all that?" Houston wonders if it would break this spell to take notes before deciding to trust his mind to lock down onto the details he needs.

"He had a steady job. He was friendly with some big-shot like you said. A producer. For a while, we both had jobs. Then, I dunno. I dunno, Lucas tried to get out. Maybe a year ago now. He said he didn't want the drugs anymore and that he could do the job without them."

"Was it just the drugs that made him quit?" Houston prompts.

"Jesus, isn't that enough? The guy said 'jump' he said 'how high'? Lucas hated it. I just..."

The junkie makes a tired gesture with his cigarette, trailing smoke in the air. "You can't just break in around here. It's just not possible. You either have money already or get in good with somebody and pray they keep interest in you, you know? Lucas had that, and he had the looks, damn him. He got a few of those Hollywood big wig types wrapped around his finger. But they did him what-for in the end; got him hooked and then strung him out."

"Why?" Houston asks, feeling a hard stone of anger forming in his gut—more than pebble-sized now but not quite enough to wrap his fist around, not quite a stone to sling just yet.

"I dunno," the junkie slurs. "Something happened. The guy came around again, right before Lucas really vanished for real, some-thing about making it up to Lucas, about bringing him back into the fold if he'd just be *reasonable*. He didn't want anything to do with me."

The junkie takes a deep, bitter breath, then plants the cigarette against his mouth again, pulls smoke and lets it out.

"Anyway, Lucas didn't talk to him. Then, he just up and vanished. Lucas, I mean. I figured he didn't have the rent and he was running out on it, but he didn't take anything."

Houston's heart struggles upward in his chest. "What did he leave?"

Gesturing around at the apartment, the junkie makes it clear how little the place has. He's sold everything that he possibly could have for his next hit. It leaves him behind in an apartment one-step-up from a cardboard box.

"Is the producer still in town?" Houston asks, focusing in on the issue at hand. It won't make him feel any better to understand the junkie, to wonder if this was what the last weeks of Lucas' life were like. He has to dig up what he can without getting trapped in the hole.

The junkie shakes his head, then hesitates before concluding, "I dunno."

"Where did Lucas sleep?" Houston asks, demanding an answer he can act on. If he has to look at this sad sap any longer, he'll fall prey to pity.

"The room in back," the junkie points vaguely toward the one short hall in the apartment.

Houston gets up, trading a look with Exeter that tells him to keep an eye on the junkie. It passes back and forth in the effortless understanding that law enforcement officials share. *Maybe a trait shared with common thugs.*

"Hey," the junkie protests weakly. "You can't—he can't—"

The protests fall on deaf ears even when he turns to Exeter. Up the hall, Houston finds three doors. One, open, leads into a dirty bathroom where brown grime has invaded every corner, over the yellow stain of cigarette smoke. On the tile wall of the shower, a healthy colony of black mold cries out for bleach.

The room on the left is little more than a square with a pile of blankets and well-abused pillows. These too show the signs of dingy neglect and an unwashed history. There are squares on the carpet where furniture once stood, and the closet door hangs open to reveal a pitiful collection of clothes on wire hangers from the cleaners.

A sour smell hangs in the air—a spoiled-milk tang that swims in through Houston's nostrils and lives at the back of his throat—a heavy weight that threatens to leave his appetite permanently crippled.

Seeing no sign of Lucas, Houston passes this room and moves up the hall. The last door is closed, and Houston tries the knob with low expectations. At least Lucas had *something* like a home, here. The journey across country must have been difficult, and the weeks leading up taxing him until his reserves were empty.

The door opens willingly, revealing an empty, white-painted room. It's the only one with a window—Houston sees some familiarity in Lucas' affinity for light, and the logic in the junkie choosing a room that would give him the most privacy possible.

Houston steps into the patch of sunlight painting the cream-and-dinge-colored carpet. It warms Houston's shoes as he stands in the last place that Lucas had once belonged. The room and the attached closet are empty from floor to ceiling.

The air is cleaner in this room. Houston closes his eyes in the abandoned space and reaches with his thoughts across time and distance. Had this ever been a safe place for Lucas—a haven built on a dream—or had it always carried the bitter taste of what it had cost him?

When he opens his eyes again he can see that in one corner the rug has been lifted away from the tack strips and hastily pushed back down. He feels the tug of curiosity against his consciousness, and the knowledge of Lucas' squirrelish tendencies. Lifting the rug, Houston finds what looks like the bare floor beneath, a section of the padding cut away and then placed back.

Crouching down, Houston lifts the corner away and back a little further, removing the padding to examine the floorboards beneath. One looks a little more obvious, a short piece that runs to the wall—loose. With the edge of a key, he pries up the short section and pulls it up to see what's beneath.

A creaking protest answers, kicking up a cloud of dust as Houston lifts the board away. Beneath, in the dusty space between the floor joists, he finds a small cigar box, held closed by a thick handful of rubber bands. Houston reaches down into the space and curls his hand around the dry, thin cedar. There's red and gold paper on all four sides advertising the brand name, and the remains of a blue paper seal long since torn open, suggesting Houston will find something other than a few stogies inside.

He turns the box over in his hands once; it's a suggestion that either Lucas left town quickly enough to abandon it, or that he intended to come back eventually and get it. Either way, the contents will tell Houston something.

He replaces the floorboard and carpet pad, then tamps the carpet back down against the tack strips with the sole of his shoe. Carrying the box, he returns to the living room, watching carefully for any sign of recognition on the junkie's face. None comes, but a suspicious hunger pops up on his features—a clear lust.

"You can't just take—" the junkie begins.

"That room," Houston cuts him off. "Did it have furniture in it?"

"Well yes, but the rent—"

"A writing desk?" Houston cuts him off again. "A maple writing desk, with a roll-top?"

"Yes," the junkie says. "How did you—"

"My father built that desk," Houston says, overriding the junkie's words a third time. This finally gets the man to shut up. "It disappeared out of my home four years ago. How much did you get for it?"

"...twenty dollars," the junkie says, with a sullen, childish shame.

"You were ripped off," Houston says. "But it probably seemed like a godsend, huh? Twenty dollars—bet you rolled in coke for a week."

The man is silent. He glances an appeal at Exeter, who gives him nothing but a stony look in return.

"You traded years of my father's passion and sweat and efforts for a fix, junkman," Houston says coldly. "The box is coming with me."

The junkie hesitates on the verge of argument. His back's so tight into the corner here that for a moment, Houston wonders if he'll put up a fight because he figures he's got nothing to lose.

"Alright," the junkie folds. "Keep it."

Houston offers him another cigarette to take the edge off, replacing the first, long since extinguished and discarded one. He's satisfied that the junkie has given them everything useful that he's going to. There is clearly no attachment between this man and Lucas. If they were ever lovers—or even friends—the drugs became more important a long time ago.

"We're done here," Houston tells Exeter, tucking the cigar box under his arm.

Exeter nods, and turns to precede him out the door.

"Hey," the junkie calls after Houston. "What about my chain?"

Houston glances up at the torn wood next to the door, then down at the dangling chain with its sad array of short screws.

"Better call your superintendent. Tell him to use the long screws next time."

◆ ◆ ◆

Outside, Exeter holds his tongue until they're almost back to the curving dirt road that will lead them down into L.A. proper. From up here, facing the city, Houston can see the movie lots scattered below. Areas tracked out and dedicated to fantasy, to creating worlds in the past and future.

He can see that all of it is a facade from this height. A painted backdrop stretched tight between a boom crane and sand bags at the bottom edge, or a thin paper front on a low, square building that could easily contain a dressed set. The very same buildings have served as saloons and Roman halls, as Martian throne rooms and moon ballrooms.

"Sorry about your father's desk," Exeter says finally. He's looking down the hill too, both of them walking on the shoulder of the road beneath the garish HOLLYWOODLAND sign, alongside a steep ravine that drops down into the foothills below. He has his hands in his pockets, and a thoughtful expression on his face.

"Don't be," Houston says, "I made all that up."

"What?" Exeter says, turning a disbelieving look on Houston.

"My father never built anything in his entire life. I lied."

Exeter pauses to look at Houston for a long time, and then down at the cigar box under his arm. He rocks back on his heels, his eyes attentive on Houston like a child waiting for an explanation of a recently witnessed magic trick.

"The desk—and all the rest of Lucas' furniture—went missing from his place right when he did," Houston says. "I never could figure out how he managed to get it all out in the space of a few hours."

"Alright," Exeter says, playing the willing pigeon.

"I saw the indents from the feet in the empty room where I found the cigar box. I figure Lucas wanted to come back—that he *meant* to, which meant his roommate took advantage of his absence and in his desperate hours unloaded all of Lucas' possessions."

"Alright, Sherlock Holmes, I'm impressed," Exeter drawls. "Why the lie?"

"He thought there might be drugs in this box. A junkman will always be suspicious of another's stash. So I parted him with the notion of ownership, which is always easier than parting a junkie with the potential contents of the box."

"Which are? Tell me we didn't go through all that for your old boyfriend's rainy-day fix?"

"I don't think so." Houston gives the cigar box a gentle shake. "No rattle."

"Well, *open* it then. Before I die of suspense."

They step off the dirt road into a pullout providing a scenic outlook over the hills to the gawkers who make it this far. Houston digs his fingers under the mass of rubber bands—a crude but tough means of security. They resist Houston's first tug, massing up together with a taut, twanging sound as he tries to pry them off.

They foil his attempt to muscle them all off at once, their combined strength more than his own. When he begins pulling the bands off one by one, Exeter holds out his hand in a request for the box.

Houston passes it over, expecting Exeter to make an attempt of bald strength against the rubber bands and wanting to see him fail. Down the road, the gravel-and-dust crunches under the tires of an as-of-yet-unseen car. Houston glances down over the side, seeing a rushing plume of dust pooling up from the lower coil of the switchback.

A sudden rubbery twang snaps Houston's attention back to the box, and Houston sees an army knife in Exeter's hand. He looks up at Houston with a proud grin on his broad features.

"You dirty cheat," Houston grumbles.

"Always be prepared," Exeter responds wryly, passing the box back.

Houston retrieves the now-free box from Exeter's meaty paw as the car rounds the bend onto the level with them. He can hear the gravel popping and crunching under the tires of the vehicle. the way the engine is roaring and straining to pull the heavy, new model car up the incline at a racing speed.

"Are you gonna open it?" Exeter prompts, sounding impatient.

"What's that guy in such a rush for?" Houston says, eyes locked on the approaching car, drawn to the wild, jerking motion of the wheels over the road, the rooster's tail of angry brown dust billowing up behind it.

Exeter looks up, following Houston's gaze to the source of his concern. For a second, they contemplate the approaching car. Houston sees the instant that the front wheels turn and the car's nose swings right toward them, showing no sign of wavering or slowing.

"Hell," Exeter breathes, bracing.

Houston shoves him, trying to put distance between their bodies so the driver can't hit both of them at once. Exeter stumbles forward, and Houston leaps backward, the loose dirt and stones turning underfoot and sending Houston stumbling over backward. His weakened shoulder jolts painfully against the ground as he drops heavily, the cigar box flies from Houston's hands before the car turns to pursue him. The big, silver grille seems to fill his vision.

He scrambles mindlessly backwards on his hands and feet, scuttling like a crab to try and get away, hoping that Exeter has avoided injury.

Then his hand comes down on air, and Houston plunges over the edge of the roadway and tumbles into the ravine. He hits the steep cliffside once, rolling as branches and brambles claw at him, falling with no handhold until he slams to a stop against a boulder at the foot of the hill, breath dashed out of him and stars reeling and twisting in front of his vision.

8.

Houston gathers himself to consciousness at the foot of the boulder, black spots dancing in front of his vision and tumbling rocks still cascading down the hillside from the ledge above—a sharp, small rain. For a second, no part of his body wants to move. His lungs are locked tight with the panicked feeling of pressure sparking an anxious feeling in his mind.

His vision still swimming, Houston coordinates his sluggish, aching limbs enough to push himself back from the rock, relieving some of the pressure on his solar plexus, and a thin trickle of air wheezes in past his stubborn diaphragm, turning into a gasp the minute the reaction clears.

He coughs—and it *hurts*—all of his body feels like it's been gone over with meat mallets. The engine above is idling now and he can hear Exeter's raised voice. A few more pebbles come sailing over the cliff, before a larger shape sails into view—the box!

Rolling over onto his front in the thorny cliffside bramble, Houston pushes himself up on hands and knees, watching the cigar box bounce once—thankfully the tiny metal catch on the lid holds it closed—and slide the rest of the way down to the deepest part of the ravine he's in. Up on his right, he can see the lower bend of the road that leads back up to the stretch of road he fell from. There's a scuffle going on up top, Exeter shouting something Houston's ringing ears can't make out.

The car doors slam with solid, ringing thuds.

"Where the hell did the other one go?" a voice demands. Houston scrambles deeper into the brush, feeling the inch-long thorns scratch lines over his sides, catch against the sleeves of his suit coat and his shirt.

"He went over the edge," a second voice answers. "Down there somewhere."

Houston goes still, holding his breath. He can just make out the edge of the cliff through a clear patch in the undergrowth, and a hatted figure peers over it and down.

"He's probably dead," the first voice says.

"Better go down and make sure. It'd bother the locals if their nice safe development suddenly *developed* strange half-dead men running out of the bushes," the second voice answers.

Houston sees the one figure fling the burning end of his cigarette dismissively down over the edge of the cliff, and then step back from the edge and out of view. The car doors slam again—once, then a second. The engine revs up and the instant he hears the car tires crunching along on the gravel above Houston scrambles toward the place the box landed for all he's worth.

He practically steps on the cigar box, and then drops down to all fours to get it. He tucks the box up under his arm, and ducks his head down and runs blind, dragging himself through the thick brush as the sound of the car's engine and the popping of rocks slows down behind him, likely scanning the ravine where he landed for signs of him.

He tries to keep as quiet as he can in the bush, to keep moving as far and as fast as he can without giving them signs of his passage. He follows the lowest point of the ravine between the curves of the switchback road and prays it will open out into the other hills below the Hollywoodland development. Behind him, the sounds of the slowly rolling tires and the engine fades, and the brush gets thicker around him—the low, scrubby trees that seem to be the norm here, growing outward in a mad tangle of branches, rather than up. He fights his way, crawling, into the space beneath one.

Body shaking with the empty-car-engine fumes of adrenaline, Houston is alert to every sound—to the rattling gasp of his breath and the small branches breaking underfoot, the way his heart is pounding like an echoing series of punches in his chest.

A low sound whirs to life in his awareness, winding up like a cicada only lower, in a more ominous key. A spike of primal fear stabs into Houston's chest, thrown from the fist of his ancestors as the rattle picks up into a solid sound.

The snake is curled at the foot of the tree—a long, fat-bodied S-shape drawing itself up into protective strike position, rattling the warning sound from the tip of its furiously vibrating tail.

Houston steps back, eyes on the snake, the red-tan speckled back and boxy viper head his father taught him to identify. It's not an Eastern Diamondback, but Houston knows better than to tangle with any rattlesnake. He backs out of the shade beneath the tree, watching every movement the snake makes.

When he's safely out of its range, he looks up—there's no sign of pursuit, and he's come farther away from the development than he thought. He can't see the road, though he's pretty sure of the direction he came from.

High in the hills above him the Hollywoodland sign looms and when Houston has his breath and bearings back, it's by this landmark he triangulates his path back to where he hopes he'll find Exeter.

His exhaustion and wariness don't lend Houston the speed his flight gave him, and by the time he begins ascending again—tensing up and going still every time a car passes—his injuries are making themselves known.

Houston reconsiders everything nice he ever thought about

California and emerges from the brush again nearly two hours later in the surprising heat of the early spring afternoon. The old wound in his shoulder hurts, too, pounding a warning through Houston's tattered frame to rely on it less.

If anyone ever sends me another Sunny California postcard, Houston thinks, darkly, *I'm going to mail them back the pieces.*

At this hour, there's traffic on the road, but all of it moves over for Houston with the respect that the very clean rich have for the homeless. His suit is torn, full of burrs and stickers and covered in patches of dirt and his own blood.

He's sure he must look half-mad. He doesn't care. He knows that Exeter is potentially injured up by the side of the roadway, or looking for Houston in return, with all these cars just passing right on by.

Before he rounds the bend in the switchback that will bring him level with the outlook he and Ex had been standing on, he presses his back against the cliff alongside the road's other side, peering cautiously around the corner.

It's an old war trick to leave an injured enemy watched in the dead man's land between the trenches—and when his friends come after him, to pick them off as they present themselves as targets. If Exeter really is up here and hurt, they could be waiting to ambush Houston.

But, the pulloff is empty. Houston can see the deep tracks veering off the road into the soft sand of the shoulder, then where the car turned around and came back down the road. Exeter is not there.

Houston follows the tire tracks around in their deep dug circle, stepping out onto the shoulder and looking at the disturbance there for signs like a hunter follows a deer. He can see the place where he and Exeter stood; there is a mass of cut rubber bands now strewn over the dirt-and-gravel like a broken bird's nest. Then, the crumbling edge of the cliff where he went over, the tire marks leading within inches of his last footprint.

After taking all this in, Houston tucks his free hand into his pocket and looks over at the side where he shoved Exeter, trying to quiet his mind enough to understand the churned up dirt. He can see where Exeter fell, where he got up again, his footprints surrounded in the scuffle by those of several other men. Houston supposes at least the two that he heard after his fall, and a driver as well.

Then the tire-tracks lead away. He can see no sign of Exeter leaving under his own power, and the knowledge solidifies in Houston like a clenched fist. *They've taken him.* Who, he isn't sure. His instincts say this is no random attack. The men came for Houston and Exeter, were racing to find them before they could leave the Hollywoodland development.

The junkie must have run to the office and called someone; someone that would be concerned about two goons asking questions. Houston can hardly even blame him—he should have known that the itch would make a junkie so desperate that he'd carry any lead he got straight to his master in the hope of a reward. A pat on the head, a couple of dollars—a prime fix, if the information was particularly good.

The California sun cooks down on Houston's neck in a beaming line, leaving the skin there feeling like cooked bacon stretched over his spine. Houston pulls in a deep breath, feeling his ribs creak in protest as the bruises on his body expand painfully over the barrel of his chest, and then lets it out.

He heads back down the road, cigar box tucked under his arm, and knows he'll have to move forward with purpose from here on out to get to the bottom of this before Exeter's time runs out.

Back at the hotel, Houston meets the uncertain gaze of the man behind the counter with enough ferocity to stifle his questions.

He knows he looks a fright, but he needs a quiet place to investigate his leads, and on his walk back home he stopped in at the store, and with the last few dollars in his wallet, purchased some clothes. Heavy cotton work pants like an average contractor, a shirt without a collar, the sort of tough clothes one could expect to get dirty. The one he's wearing is a loss, and what he's purchased is an improvement even if it is secondhand and shabby workman's clothes.

"Sir, your check cleared," the desk-clerk says sliding Exeter's crumpled bills back over the counter toward Houston, who pockets them. Surely, Exeter won't mind the loan.

"Thanks," Houston tells him, looking him dead in the beady eyes and leaving him with whatever scandalous things he might need to think as explanation for Houston's current appearance.

Upstairs he washes his face, runs the washcloth over his neck and bruised chest, under his armpits to get the worst of the stink out. He can count his impacts with the cliffside in a satellite of bruises on the trunk of his body, and the stinging scratches of the aggressive desert plant life are too numerous to number, with several on his hands still oozing blood.

After brief consideration for salvageability, he throws the whole of his torn up and filthy suit into the trashcan under the bathroom sink to be collected by the maid. He sets the cigar box on the bed as he quickly dresses in his new clothes, then picks it up again.

He checks Exeter's room on the off-chance. It's empty and looks abandoned. Neither of them had any luggage to begin with, so there are no signs other than the used toiletries in the bathroom, the yet-to-evaporate water on the curtain in the shower.

"Hell," Houston says. He returns to his own room and upends the cigar box onto the bed. He's been holding it like a talisman since he picked it up in the ravine, without yet looking in it.

Inside he finds a thin stack of letters, rubber-banded together.

Check stubs, too, grimy from being shuffled around for a while but in order by date when Houston flips the stack. They detail six years of Lucas' employment life, held together with a crumbling rubber band that has dried out in California's heat.

Scattered among the papers are a couple of keys, one to Houston's old apartment, and another smaller one as if for a locker. Houston recognizes the code at the top, and when he flips the key over, the grip is imprinted with CHICAGO CENTRAL STATION. *Why did Lucas leave the keys, if he intended to return to Chicago?*

There's a bag with a grimy white residue, a ring, a few other small precious trinkets. Houston spreads this pitiful arrangement out on the bed and considers what it tells him.These are the last secrets that Lucas kept in a life full of secrets and artful misdirection.

Houston reaches for the letters first. He finds one in his own handwriting from the year after he returned from war. He already knew Lucas, but his hand was still spidery and nervous at the time, still showing the signs of the shellshock he'd suffered in the aftermath. He finds a couple of other letters that he doesn't recognize from the same time-period, dated by the postal validation stamps and the stamps used to send the letters.

Though Exeter's dire situation means he should set this aside and dig deeper, Houston opens the one from himself and looks it over. He doesn't remember writing the lines of clumsy poetry beyond the sensation of sitting at the table in his kitchen with the window light of early morning illuminating his hand and his cup of coffee, the soft feel of velvet paper under his sensitive fingertips.

The lines are practically nonsense to his eyes, a sort of dangerous spouting of affection that one could get away with in the past but not now. He folds the letter back into its paper shell like placing a dead snail back into its old home and leaving it to rot. Then he picks the stack up again, checking return addresses until he finds a familiar name.

T.J. Williams. It's dated to the period just after Lucas' disappearance from Chicago, and Houston sets it aside, sorting out several others that come from the same mailing address, and then—he discovers two that come from the man's home, he'd guess. This is not the care of address of a company, not official communications.

The first is a stock letter congratulating Lucas on his acceptance to the production Houston found his name billed in, and he scans it, finding that it's typed except for the signature at the bottom, scrawled in a heavy hand in fading blue ink – the cheap kind they sell for a nickel, without lightfastness. There are smudges from repeated reading on the letter, the signs of hope that it brought to the recipient, and Houston looks it over three times to see if there's any sign of the future that awaited, the trap that was about to spring.

There's nothing but the tame language of promise without the strong words of commitment. *Selected*, it says, and *second audition*, and a date and place in Hollywood to report. It's a backlot, Houston notices, private and away from prying eyes. There were probably enough legitimate auditions held under such conditions so as not to arouse even the first hint of suspicion.

The last letter has an L.A. address on Sunset where Houston would bet T.J. Williams still keeps his offices. It's dated the previous November. Houston can't bring himself to let go of the case now that it's all coming together. Lines from here to Chicago, running straight and parallel like train tracks. If asking questions about Lucas' disappearance and how it tied to T.J. Williams brought trouble down on them that fast, Houston can bet Williams is the one who has Ex's fate in his hands. Maybe this address is still the one he uses now—a lead to Ex's wearabouts.

He unfolds the letter inside. There's several individually folded pages, all handwritten, and Houston wonders how a career blackmailer could put so much ammunition into the letter. Scanning it over, Houston finds it's hardly poetry—instead, it's a lurid and grotesque detailing of a party and an evening of congress that makes Houston feel ill. The tone of the letter is taunting and superior, lording the power Williams claimed to have over Lucas.

When he reaches the last page, a small section of film falls out, clipped from a larger reel. Houston catches it and holds it up to the light from the window. It's three frames in close-up, and it's enough . All bare skin, one clear face, and no art in it. Houston knows Lucas too well not to recognize him even in filthy miniature and celluloid.

A low, roiling upset rises in Houston's belly, raising the barometric pressure of his anger.

The letter promises better parts in the future—and plenty of favors, so long as Lucas continued to oblige Williams with his body. Promises retribution if he doesn't fall in line. It describes the use of drugs in slowly building quantities, too. *Was Lucas unwilling to take them, at first?*

Houston sets the letter aside for a moment and takes a deep breath. It's all connected and he's sure now that if he finds Williams he'll find answers—and Exeter. The sooner the better. He scoops all of the unrelated items back into the cigar box and hides it between the mattress and bedframe.

Houston folds the letter back together, stuffing the entire bundle of letters from Williams into his pocket. Then, on second thought, he pulls a few of them back out, and repacks them with the strip of film into a hotel stationary envelope, hastily making the front out to Sal with the clerk's skipping desk pen. He pays for a stamp and asks for the letter to be mailed immediately.

On the street, Houston pauses to use the phone booth, making the connection to Chicago by memory, and asking for his building.

"Hello, thank you for calling the Carlin building." Miss Wentz's familiar accent shakes Houston a little, making him feel out of synchronization with the place he's standing. Lost in time and place and far from where he belongs.

"How may I direct your call?"

"Miss Wentz, this is Houston Mars,"

"Huey!" she exclaims, making him wince. "Honey, are you okay? I haven't seen you all week, and Mr. Costanzo is worried sick."

"I'm alright," Houston assures her. He's not sure he is, not completely, but there's no reason to worry her unnecessarily. "I'm just taking care of some business out of town."

"Oh, I'm glad," she breathes a small, sweet sigh. "I was pretty worried too. You never miss so much work."

Houston doesn't feel that way about it. He's been working the whole time, nose to the grindstone on a case. He realizes he has more to tell Sal about his lead, too.

"Is Sal still working that case from last week?" Houston asks, feeling a momentary twinge of guilt for running out on his partner.

"Yeah, I think so," Miss Wentz says. "He's been in and out a lot."

"Is he in right now?"

"I'm not sure, Huey," she says. "Want me to ring you up there?"

"Please."

"One moment, please," she says, slipping her courtesy on like a very lovely glove. Houston hangs on the line before he connects to the office upstairs.

The phone rings twice before Sal answers, "Detective agency."

"Sal." Houston is glad to hear his voice. He knows what he has to say, what he needs to tell his partner about but there is a lot unsaid that he should cover, and enough attachment between them that to launch straight into business without addressing it would be damaging. "Sorry I left without telling you. I... got a lead."

"Houston? Christ. Where are you?" Sal demands. "I've been all over the city. I've been feeding your damn cat."

Shit. Houston realizes he forgot all about Chop Suey.

"Thanks," Houston manages.

"Where *are* you?" Sal repeats in a different tone.

"I'm in Los Angeles," Houston reveals, feeling a guilty tide overcoming him. "I got a tip to look into something down here, and I had to see if it would pan out."

"Los Angeles?" Sal repeats, sounding dazed. "You're nuts, Houston. What are you doing in California?"

"It turns out I've got a lead on T.J. Williams," Houston explains, "and it goes back to Lucas, too."

"What?"

"I think this guy's been running the scheme for years, and he roped in guys from Chicago before. I found another one of his blackmail letters in Lucas' place here."

There's a long moment before Sal responds. "Houston—*Hobbes*—you don't have the resources to go after those people. You're gonna get hurt out there."

The sign of concern reaches into Houston and startles him, the sort of bald worry for each other that they usually don't display openly.

"I got even worse news for you," Houston says. "Ex is here—or he was—and while we were looking into this, they grabbed him. I don't know where he is."

"What are you saying?"

"Some guys ran us off the road, and they took Ex." Houston realizes that's barely coherent, and he stops to take a breath. He realizes he can taste the city around him, the heat-cooked concrete and sunscreen that seems baked into the very air. It brings to light the differences between L.A. and his darker, colder home.

"Exeter is there?" Sal asks.

"You sent him after me," Houston says. "I guess he took that pretty serious."

"No," Sal says, stopping Houston from going on a tirade. "A week ago, I asked him if he'd seen you around. He said no, he was working on something for Dan O'Halloran—"

"*Dan O'Halloran?*" Houston exclaims, suddenly angry. *Did Ex lie to me?* "Exeter's been babysitting me this whole time. I thought you sent him."

"I never asked him to do that. Christ—and you're saying someone's kidnapped him? How?"

"When they came at us in the car, I went over a cliff." Houston sounds crazy even to himself. "Ex didn't, and I guess they grabbed him."

"Shit," Sal says, sounding angry, and very far away. "Are you alright? What are you gonna do about it?"

"I'm going after him," Houston says, realizing only as he says it that's what he intends to do. "I have to get Ex back, and if I get to the bottom of this, I'm sure I'll find him. Listen, I sent you a letter—"

"Would you call the cops, *please*?"

"I should," Houston admits. He hesitates, knowing he probably won't until there's no other option. If Sal knows him at all, he knows the truth, too. For a long moment, they are both quiet on the line.

"I'm getting on a plane," Sal says.

"You can't afford that."

"I can if I ask my *family*."

Houston rocks back on his heels, pulling in a breath at the proposition. Sal hates going to his family for dirty money as a matter of pride, but Houston knows if the shoe were on the other foot and it was Sal out here, he'd beg borrow or steal to close the gap. It feels strangely heavy in his chest.

"You'll be too late." Houston stirs back to action, shifting his weight. "Watch out for the letter. I'll get back in touch, Sal."

"Don't bother," Sal says, with an angry lightness to his tone. "I'm coming to you."

"Alright," Houston says, and the word hangs. He puts the phone up after a long moment without saying goodbye.

9.

Sunset Boulevard at noontime is a choked miasma of cars and tan bodies. This part of the strip contains all of the offices of representatives and agents for the lots scattered around town, and Houston can see all the hopeful faces—some young, some a little older, some refined—others without a hope in the world except maybe to break it big so they didn't have to return to Nebraska and starve to death quietly.

Houston keeps his hands in his pockets, aware of the bundle of letters in his back pocket, opposite his wallet. He wonders if he should have a gun. Maybe Exeter is carrying his sidearm, maybe he's already out of captivity, but Houston bets he'd have used it in the initial conflict if he was going to use it at all.

Instead he supposes he'll rely on his wits and what parts of combat training still stay with him. *If only I had a bayonet, now....*

He finds the office he's looking for behind it's very own line of transplanted palm trees, reaching up skyward and drifting against the blue heavens, perfectly spaced as if waiting for film themselves. The tops look precariously balanced on the thin trunks, wavering and uncertain, as if any heavy breeze could come and topple them—and yet they stand on, isolated towers of improbable solidity. Somehow, even though the country has begun to starve, these aliens have been watered and cared for, nursed up the way that middle America could so badly use.

Houston checks the street address against the top envelope in his pocket. The building itself is some kind of bungalo, a series of offices in a building that was informal, like a house. It has a low slanting roof made out of corrugated tin and painted red to look like terracotta tiles. sandwiched onto a boxy stucco frame with odd shapes plunging off, and an uneven front. It looks like a giant's hand has punched the front of the building in the middle, creating a depression between the two large eyes of it's windows, where the inset mouth of the doorway is. Like one of those cats or dogs with the faces shoved in so far it was a wonder they didn't have teeth sticking out of the backs of their heads.

Houston steps through the building's front entrance and into the open courtyard. Like so many things in Hollywood, the front is only a facade for the interior, which opens into a u-shaped courtyard that's open on the far end and surrounded by doors leading into separate offices. At the center there is thick grass and a water fountain in the middle of it. It provides a constant trickle just audible enough to tantalize the bladder, dribbling water over a curved series of bowls—from a tiny one at the very top down the progression of sizes and into a tiled basin that's inset into the ground. It cools the immediate area, but leaves the air heavy and humid, thick to breathe.

He passes the doors to the other offices that encircle the courtyard, until he's sure he has the right one—T.J. Williams' name is on a worn brass plaque next to the door, artificially aged to give it a venerable look. There's a five pointed star beneath it, and the words 'Executive Agent & Producer' appended below in smaller text. A big bay window to the left of the door looks out into the centralized courtyard, but it's shuttered with dusty white venetian blinds—the slats neglected by the janitor or whatever cleaning service they have in this place.

Behind the door, he finds a waiting room, with three hopefuls —all young men—sitting in the chairs along one wall. Houston can see they have blond hair, wholesome faces, lean bodies. They're young—younger than Lucas was when he came to Hollywood. They have unlined faces that suggest they might even still be teenagers, but no older than their twenties. These are boys that haven't seen war, though they might yet.

"We don't take walk-ins," a woman's voice tells Houston, and he turns from the line of hopeful faces—the boys now eyeing him suspiciously as if he were an out of place wrinkle on a starched suit.

He turns to the source of the voice, a secretary behind the desk. She's wearing a powder-pink dress that hugs every line of her trim, curvy body. It's an effort at beauty that's cultured to pull the eye, though Houston doesn't feel the weight of the effect. Her eyes are hard, ice-chip blue, and her hair is tucked up into a bun at the back of her head without a strand out of place. It's color is a red that could only come out of a bottle and must be layered on top of her natural blonde; she has light eyebrows.

Houston tucks his hands politely behind his back and rocks back on his heels. "I'm Detective Mars, ma'am. I've got a few questions for Mr. Williams."

"We're not expecting any detective," the secretary says. Next to a vase of fresh flowers, there's a small plaque—fake wood-grain with white letters that slide on between a set of rails on the top and bottom. Houston supposes something so interchangeable might be practical if Williams can't keep a secretary for long. It currently reads "Shirley," and Houston hopes it's been changed recently.

"Remember, Shirley? We spoke on the phone, ma'am," Houston says, keeping his hands tamely behind his back. He looks at her, meeting her stoney-hard and defensive gaze and wonders what brought her to L.A. Was she once a hopeful, too? Does she still hope—have that little dream that one day, T.J. Williams will walk out of his office and see his secretary with her perfectly pink dress and her matching nails—these beautifully mani- cured and resting on the keys of her typewriter as if she knows truly what to do with it—and realize he's had a star, right there, right under his nose the whole time?

Houston doubts it; he suspects if Williams notices her at all, it's because she is tempting bait to set out for his investors.

"We most certainly did not," she says sharply. Not the sort of woman to have a phone conversation and forget about it. "Now you go on out of here. I've heard every trick in the book and Mr. Williams won't have any of it. If you don't have an appointment, don't even bother!"

Houston shows his P.I. license, hoping she won't read too closely. She leans in, and works her eyes over the first few lines, then sits back and looks up as if to measure Houston against the description provided. *So much for that.*

"You're not with the police."

"No ma'am, I'm looking into private affairs on behalf of the estate of Mr. Harcourt," Houston bluffs, watching her for signs of recognition.

"Who?" she asks. Houston can't tell if the reaction is genuine. Perhaps Mr. Williams has a lot of clients, perhaps the secretary is a relatively new recruit.

"One of Mr. William's clients," Houston explains. He raises his voice a little, pitching it to catch the attention of the three fellows behind him. "Turned up dead under suspicious circumstances just after Christmas."

When he's sure he has their attention, he raises his voice just a little further. "Mr. Williams is one of his last known contacts."

Shirley glances over her shoulder toward one of the two closed doors behind her, tellingly. Houston goes toward it, without waiting for further invitation.

"Don't you dare," she starts, but he gets a hand on the doorknob before she can get to her feet and block his path. He swings the door open and bulls his way into the office with Shirley hot on his heels, plucking at the sleeve of his shirt."

"What on earth?" a man's voice demands. "Shirley!"

Shirley leans in around Houston's shoulder. "I'm sorry, Mr. Williams, he just barged in. He says he's some kind of detect-"

"I have some questions for you," Houston cuts in on his own behalf.

"I'm not seeking unsolicited talent at this time," Williams says, looking up from his desk at the scene taking place in his doorway, wearing a faintly annoyed expression on his broad, clean-shaven features. He doesn't have anyone else in the office, and doesn't seem to be expecting anyone, despite the young men in the waiting room. He sets his pen down flat on his desk with a motion that implies finality.

"I'm not talent," Houston says, flatly. "I'm here about Lucas Harcourt."

He watches Williams' expression change slowly from exasperation to guarded reserve.

"I'm sorry, sir," Shirley says, around Houston's shoulder. "Do you want me to call security?"

"No, thank you, Shirley," Williams says. "I'll handle this."

Inside T.J. William's office, the walls are covered in framed movie posters, with the occasional autographed copy interspersed on productions he must have been instrumental in. The desk dominates one side of the room, and the window Houston saw from the courtyard dominates the wall behind it, shuttered over with it's slatted shade. He can see a glimpse of the courtyard beyond and hear the faint trickling of the fountain.

Houston closes the door between them and Shirley. With Williams' eyes on him warily, he crosses the thick carpet and drops down into the chair on the near side of Williams' desk. He pulls out his battered pack of Chesterfields and. at a glance around, sees no sign of an ashtray or the signs of a habitual smoker. There are other vices in evidence—a fully stocked bar cart, and of course, the letters in Houston's pocket.

He lights up anyway, despite Williams' warning glare.

"Don't smoke in here. It's a vile habit," Williams says.

Houston silently appraises him as he takes his first long puff, raking his eyes over Williams' form. He is broad-shouldered but with severe features badly fit onto a broad face. He'd be tall, standing. Houston thinks he looks like a priest or a pastor, but stretched out into a broad caricature. He has a long nose jabbing out from his face like an echo to a pointing finger over a pulpit. His small eyes are fixed acutely on Houston with anger, seeming bright from deep in their sockets. The hairline on his head has begun to creep back irregularly, leaving him with an off-centered widow's peak that he grooms back. Houston wonders if he's proud of it, if he takes it as a sign of distinguished age.

"You know what else is a vile habit?" Houston asks, exhaling smoke into the atmosphere of the room to test Williams patience. The nicotine seems to charge him, easing vitality back into his aching muscles.

For a moment, he thinks that Williams might shout for his secretary to come and remove Houston from the room. Williams isn't shaken, he's secure there behind his desk, clearly feeling like he's a king behind the wall. He hasn't put together why Houston is here; it's just one more rude annoyance in his day.

"Raping the young men in your employ," Houston finishes his thought, keeping his posture as calm and easy as he can. "Forcing them to give you sexual favors in return for minor parts in your two-bit productions. I'd say that's a pretty vile habit."

Williams is silent for a long moment, the coal-bright fire in his piggy eyes burning bright. Houston is utterly repulsed by him, this ugly man who would turn against his own and seek to punish them for ambition, get his own sick relief whatever way he could and probably think of it as a victory.

"What's the matter? You think it's a *nice* thing you do?" Houston says. "Not a single woman out there in the room, aside from that new secretary you've got. I wonder why that is? What happened to the last one? She get wind of your disgusting games and make for the hills, or did you do it to her too, until she'd had enough and got out of this town?"

"You're a madman," Williams spits after his long, desperate silence. "Who do you think you are, coming in here? I don't know you from Adam, and you're making these—these horrific accusations. Why, I should call the police! I should have you thrown in jail for slander! Who do you *think*—"

"I'm Houston Mars," Houston says, cutting off Williams' tirade with a low, warning tone. He stands up suddenly, cigarette still clenched in his hand. He's holding it so hard between his fisting fingers that it breaks at the filter and the whole burning front end of it falls to the eggshell colored carpet and begins to burn a hole through the plush strands. Houston ignores it, letting the smoke pour up in thin wisps as if the fires of hell are coming to life beneath them. "You sent men after my partner this morning, because you thought we were getting too close. Your little dog out at the Stay-A While called you—you hole up all your boys out there? Did you fuck his room-mate too, or was that just for Lucas?"

Now, Williams is silent, and Houston put his hands flat on the man's desk, leaning over it and stepping to one side as the carpet begins to smoulder up into little flames, the mixed fabric melting and blackening in small patches as embers fly up and land in new places.

"Now you listen to me, you sick son of a bitch," Houston says, keeping his tone as quiet as confessional on Sunday, even and level despite the way his insides are a roiling firestorm of anger and resentment. He wants to haul his fist back and smash this man's teeth in; to drag him over his own desk and push his face down in the burning carpet until his scars would render him as ugly outside as his soul is. "You better tell me where they took Exeter, and then you better think about taking yourself down to the police station and confessing what kind of sadistic sodomist you are because the only place–the *only* place—you'll ever be safe from me is in jail."

"You can't—" Williams starts, beady eyes darting between Houston looming over him and the burning carpet. "This isn't true. None of it is true, and you can't even begin to prove it. Why, who would admit to—"

Houston produces the bundle of Lucas' letters from his pocket, and slaps them onto the desk in front of Williams; the weight of his sins against the feather on the scales and it's clear by his expression he knows which way they're tipping.

"Lucas was smarter than you," Houston says. "He didn't deserve what you did to him, but you're sure going to deserve what you have coming."

Williams' eyes go hard, giving his face a mean and focused expression, turning on Houston like the double barrels at the end of a shotgun. All of the fear and outrage drains out of his features after a moment, and instead a slow smile creeps madly over his features.

"You brought it right to me," Williams says as the smoke begins to really fill the room. "You're that idiot they drove off a cliff this morning."

Houston gives him a moment to let him think he's won, and holds his tongue. He has the long play in reserve, but takes comfort in knowing it. That no matter what the events of the next few moments, he'll be alright in the end. Some of the Letters are already on the way back to Chicago, hopefully parts that are important enough to do something with.

"Alright, Mr. Mars," Williams says. "What exactly do you plan to do with all this 'evidence'? Your star witness died three months ago in Chicago."

The words burn. Houston resists the urge to punch him just to shut him up. There's still time for them to make the hard deal; to get Exeter back before he's damaged irreparably.

"I came to play ball, Williams," Houston says. "Trade you what

you want in exchange for the whereabouts of my partner—
alive."

"I wouldn't begin to know where he is now," Williams bluffs.

Houston lunges across the desk as his self control snaps at last,
displacing the letters off the side. The office is full of smoke
now, and any second it will begin to leak under the door, or the
smell of burning polyester will summon the secretary from her
desk and into the middle of the conflict. She'll call the police,
probably. Nice sensible girl.

He curls his hands under Williams' lapels and yanks him out
of his seat so they're face to face. "You get your goons on
the phone, Williams, and you get Exeter here in the next five
minutes or so help me you and I will both stand here until
this whole place burns down and I'll *watch* as the devil himself
comes up to claim you like Don Giovanni."

Williams finally hits him then, bunching up his doughy fist and
levering it up under Houston's sternum, slamming the breath
out of him. It surprises him that Williams has the capacity
at all, and Houston stumbles backwards without giving up his
hold, dragging Williams over the desk.

They both hit the floor in a heap on the other side, smoke stinging Houston's eyes as he scrambles to fight back—give as good
as he gets. He can hear that their scuffle has attracted attention.
Shirley's voice shouts at them to stop, but Houston won't give
up his hold.

There's heat on the back of his head and Houston rolls away
from the burning swath of carpet. The impact has locked the
breath out of Houston's chest. He cocks his fist back and jams
it into Williams' teeth as the man fights to get out of his hold.
There's a satisfying impact of knuckles on bone. He rolls them
both over, slamming Williams down onto the burning hole
spreading rapidly over the office floor. Suddenly, the fire seems
bigger, licking at the desk and surrounding them as they roll and

pitch on the floor.

Williams' suit is burning as he hits Houston again, connecting with his jaw hard enough to rattle him. The pain clarifies Houston's thoughts enough to worry about the bundle of envelopes on the—*burning!*—floor, imperiled as much as he and Williams are. His head has begun to swim with the smoke; the air feeling hot and thin when his lungs unlock at last and he can gasp it in. He kicks Williams off him just as the man seems to realize his suit is on fire.

Instead of doing anything sensible, Williams begins swatting at the burning wool, while Houston gets carefully up onto his hands and knees, searching for his bearings. In the scuffle, they've kicked over the bar cart, upsetting the decanters of alcohol onto the carpet. The spill is now feeding the blaze. Houston makes no effort to put it out, hearing the secretary yelling into the phone for the fire department and the front door of the office slamming as the waiting room clears out.

Houston spots the packet of letters under the burning wood of the desk, and grabs for it. He beats it out with his palms frantically, trying to smother the embers burning along the edge of the bundle. Finally he throws off his shirt and does his best to smother the bundle, wrapping it all together against his chest and lunging for the exit.

Williams is screaming now, and Houston can smell burning hair. He turns in the doorway to see that Williams has put his foot in the burning alcohol and it's soaked his pants-cuff and begun to burn more intensely. Houston gets ahold of himself enough to realize something has to be done, but he doesn't see any obvious way to put Williams out.

"For the love of god, isn't there some water?" Houston barks at Shirley, where she stands frozen with the phone receiver in her hand, staring wide-eyed and open mouthed at the image in front of her.

"It's," she starts in a small voice, turning her wide-eyes wildly over the room as if seeking a source of water in the desert.

"A bucket, with water in it!" Houston roars, as Williams stumbles against the picture window, tearing down the blinds. He's more on fire than not, now.

"Sir, you're-" Shirley starts, and then Houston has to drop the smouldering bundle in his arms, ripping the flower vase off her desk and upending it unthinkingly over the shirt. The embers burning through promptly go out, and Houston can hear distant sirens. Williams is still screaming, terrible yelping cries as he thrashes helplessly. The heat of the flames from the office washes over Houston, then the sound of crashing glass pulls his attention up from the pile of ruined evidence and sopping flowers at his feet. He looks up to see that Wiliams has thrown himself through the thick glass of the window, tumbling through onto the grass outside. *Is he going for the fountain?*

As the office goes up in flames, Houston swings his arm around Shirley's shoulders and drags her along with him, away from the flames. She seems shocky and speechless, unable to tear her wide, glassy eyes away from Williams' flight. Houston stops only long enough to grab his sopping shirt and the enclosed letters within, hooking his burned hand through the strap of her purse to pull it out from under the desk. He puts it into her hands and pushes her out the door and along the hall past the main entrance to the street where it's safe.

Houston's last sight before he tears himself away is of Williams hopping through the grass and stripping off his clothes, suit and hair ablaze, his helpless hands red and blistered as he runs toward his hope of salvation.

10.

"**O**h my word," Shirley is repeating, clutching her purse as he steers her across the street to safety. "Oh my *word!*"

Houston guesses she's not going to care much for Hollywood or secretary work after this anyway. She looks lost and afraid as he guides her behind the safety lines the firemen are setting up to guide the trucks in. They wrench the seal off the hydrant and join the hose onto it, scrambling around efficiently to assess the fire.

Houston leaves her in the crowd and slips away, around to the back of the building facing the courtyard.

In a scorched patch of grass, he finds the remains of T.J. Williams. The body is still moving, still burning and smoking, but Houston knows a dead man when he sees one. He was brought such shelled out husks of men, and knows that the shock will finish it if the smoke hasn't ruined Williams' lungs already. There's only instinct left in this creature, though he probably can't see the fountain anymore. There's little recognizable of him, and Houston knows well the scent of scorched fat and burnt wool, the rattling sound of his wheeze. In the war, he found the sight of such men pitiable; here he feels nothing—not triumph and only faint remorse.

He crouches next to the specter. "Williams. Tell me where they took my partner this morning. You're not going to jail, but you could do one worthwhile thing. Save one man so they'll weigh your soul a little less heavy."

Williams only croaks with his burned out voice box, and manages to crawl another inch on his belly, like the serpent in Eden.

Houston goes to the fountain in the center of the yard, sits down, and pulls out a cigarette. After several failed attempts with his soggy all-weather matches, he lights it. Houston watches Williams expire in the grass, and tries to feel out the bigger picture as the thinning smoke wafts by and stings his eyes. His own hands are burnt and tender from retrieving the letters, and his crumpled up shirt leaves a wet patch over his lap as he observes. No devil from hell comes up to claim the man, no promise of the real punishment or atonement he deserves, he just transforms from a living human to burning meat, the staple of every wholesome barbeque across the country. The air fills with the smell of wet, soaking smoke, growing heavy with the water the fire truck is pouring in long arcs over the burning office. For a long moment, Houston and the remains are alone, and he tries to feel some satisfaction in it.

When he's finished his cigarette he puts out the butt end in the fountain, and finds the surface of the green, sluggishly moving water already flecked with ash. All of the attention is still on the front of the buildings, so he goes easily out through the alleyway behind the Sunset offices onto the next street over, and back into the depths of Hollywood.

Behind him, the burning plume of smoke rises, black and dark with anger for being extinguished.

Houston's hands blister quickly, but he's not concerned for their function. The left is worse than the right, and his clothes started the day second-hand and now are ready for the dump. They've only been in his possession for a few hours, but since he's started working this case he's burned through things like clothes and people in record time.

Lungs aching from the smoke, and head spinning with events, Houston stops in a diner and takes a coffee, unfolding the singed and soaked package of letters across the table with hesitation.

Most of the ink has smeared and run completely off the page or soaked into other parts of the folded papers. The corners of the envelopes are blackened, leaving Houston with little more than damp, washed-out and crumbling remains. The man he might have used them against is now dead, but this is all that remained of Lucas' last years, the time of his life Houston has no other way of knowing about, so he's reluctant to surrender the soggy, illegible mess they've become.

When the waitress comes to refill his coffee cup, she frowns sympathetically at him. "Aw, hon. You look like you've been through hell."

Houston supposes he has. The little bit of human sympathy is enough to penetrate the haze. "Hell's not so bad. I was in the war, too."

She pats him gently on the shoulder. "Listen, honey, it's none of my business, but whoever the letters were from—they understand. Just tell her you're sorry you lost them."

Houston keeps his hands hidden in his lap and wonders what she thinks his story is. *Some poor sot who fell asleep half drunk with a cigarette in his hand?* He doesn't have the heart to tell her the truth. He settles for a sorry half-measure. "I wish I could."

It surprises him how much he means it. When she brings him the trash can, he pushes the soggy mess of letters into it, forcing himself to let go. He finishes his coffee and empties his wallet onto the table before he leaves the diner, wondering how the hell he's supposed to find Exeter.

Williams wasn't in this alone. Obviously, he had support, was running a partly legitimate business as a lure and the rest was on the side. Someone is in Chicago on his behalf—or he was on someone *else's* behalf. Who is running the show? He tries to think back to the details of the porno case Sal picked up. The precipice he's lept off to bring him here. *What was it Sal said?*

A twinge of guilt accompanies the thought. Houston stands here, all alone in L.A. He's lost Exeter—possibly gotten him *killed*—and left Sal behind, plowing his past through the bricks and mortar of his present like a wrecking ball. He's stepped out on everything, and briefly, achingly, he remembers what it's like to be on the other end of that. *That moment where I woke up, and I knew he was really gone.*

He paws for a cigarette and finds the pack as empty as his pockets. Houston crumples it up and jams it back into his jeans pocket. *It must be someone with the ability to pull strings like this. Who could take a small-time pornographer and blackmailer and put them in an office on Sunset Boulevard? Hard to keep the Mob out.* The thought triggers a memory. *Shit.*

Williams didn't keep the Mob out in the end. They came in—maybe just because he was operating on their turf, maybe Williams did something so stupid as to borrow money, but then they had him. Took over and expanded, and now they're protecting some lucrative part of their operation. And *they* have Exeter.

The idea forms slowly, recklessly in his mind. Houston stands on Hollywood Boulevard with his hands twitching for a cigarette as the evening begins to wash over the city, and the sign in the hills above comes on and begins to pound out it's merciless pulse along its lighted letters over and over.

HOLLY – WOOD – LAND.

It's dark when he steps onto the road that will take him back up into the hills, and by the time he makes it back to the Sta-A-While it's full night. Houston faces down the junkie's door again and feels his veins filled with smoke and fire. He begins to pound on the door.

"What?" the junkie's voice answers cautiously from inside. "No, *you* go away! I have nothing more for you!"

Houston kicks the door in.

"Go on, call them," Houston growls as the junkie cowers on the floor of his empty apartment. There's only one lamp with a single bulb burning a tired circle against the darkness that otherwise fills the space. "Get ahold of your Mafia buddies again. I need to talk to them."

"I don't know what you're talking about," the junkie cries. "Please, I wish I'd never met you, get out of here!"

Houston crouches down, knowing he looks a wreck and a biblical liar with his burned hands. He drapes his elbows on his knees, making sure to look the man in his eyes. There's a tight feeling in his jaw, and an anger inside him like galloping horses.

"I know you called them this morning," Houston snarls. "I know you told them that my partner and I were looking into this, hoping you'd get some reward. That someone would pat you on the head like a dog. You called Williams himself, maybe. People came after us."

The junkie shakes his head weakly, chin quivering, and for that instant, Houston hates him more than he's ever hated anyone. He could own up to the chaos he's caused, or he could have taken this morning's warning as an opportunity to get out. Instead, here he still is, useless and terrified.

"Williams is dead you little punk," Houston tells him, hoping to shake some sense into him. "And my partner is still missing. So you call the goons you called this morning and get them back here. Tell them I came back and I'm waiting for them. Tell them their boss is dead. Whatever it takes to get them back here."

"I don't have…" the junkie starts moving slowly, to pick himself up, eyes darting for the door behind Houston. He moves like an animal with a light in its eyes, as if waiting for permission. Of course he doesn't have a phone, but he made contact that morning somehow.

"The phone is in the clubhouse," the junkie explains. "I'd have to go and..."

Houston doesn't trust the man but there's at least one part of the statement that's obviously true. "Let's go."

"Go?"

"Phone's in the clubhouse. You'll need it." Houston seizes the junkie by the upper arm and hauls him to his feet. He marches the junkie down to the clubhouse at the center of the housing complex. There's a phone booth mounted along the outside wall, with a clean, efficient look to it. A sort of chic camouflage. Houston shoves the junkie in, shuts the door behind him, and waits just outside.

The junkie pats his dirty jeans down in obvious search for change. Houston watches him dispassionately until he comes up with a begrudging dime, slots it into the phone tab and dials the exchange by memory. Houston takes notes of the numbers. After a few rings, the phone connects.

"F-fellas," the junkie stutters into the phone. Houston's not sure if he's more worried about Houston or whoever he's talking to. "Can you put Scotty on? I got something important for him."

Houston can't hear the other end of the conversation, but the junkie's eyes dart toward him, nervously, as if any delay will send Houston off the deep end. *It just might.*

Houston considers the options laid out before him like the picked-over remains of a buffet reaching the end of its viable lifespan. He's not sure what to do beyond this wild bid for contact. If he hadn't failed so spectacularly with Williams, he wouldn't be in this situation. More importantly, Ex has been in their custody for a number of hours now. Each has increased the likelihood of irreversible harm, especially if the news of William's death—on whose orders Exeter is presumably held—has reached the henchmen before Houston's taunt. If it has, he has to face the very real possibility that his move could have caused harm to his erstwhile partner.

He can chastise himself for it later if it becomes the case. In the meantime, while there's any chance of success—it takes precedence that he locates Ex by any means left to him, including antagonism.

"You let one get away this morning," the junkie says after a pause. He keeps one eye nervously on Houston. Sweat stands out on his brow in the dim glow of the building's porch light. He pauses to listen and then continues. "He's *here* at my apartment, you asshole. He's saying Williams is dead!"

A response, and then the junkie, with his eyes on Houston as if watching for a telegraph signal that he's about to make the wrong move, continues. "*Yes,* now. If you hurry—"

The junkie slams the receiver back into the phone cradle. Houston steps back from the booth doors. "Are they coming?"

"Either they are or they aren't. I'm not sure if Scotty thought… anyway, if they think it's their problem, they'll come." The junkie presses forward, pushing the door against Houston in an effort to get past. He carries with him a stale cloud of his body odor and fresh, sour sweat. "Now let me out of here, huh? I did what you wanted me to, you maniac."

He has, but Houston still hesitates, he's not sure whether it's on the point of warning the guy to get some help or because if this doesn't work, this sad-sack is still his best hope of making a connection.

Finally, he decides. "They're coming. Get out of here."

When he steps aside, the junkie blows past him and away from the complex. He casts only one frantic, wild glance back over his shoulder at Houston. Houston stands up straighter and wishes he had a cigarette to keep him company while he waits for trouble to come to him.

Back at the junkie's apartment, he investigates the place signs of a useful weapon. It's a simple layout, the whole space a boxy rectangle running front to back. The front door opens between the empty living room on one side and an open archway into a ramshackle kitchen on the other side. When the front door is open, it blocks the kitchen entryway.

It's too much to hope that there might be a gun—and Houston's a lousy shot anyway—in fact, he can't even find a carving or butter knife. There's no frying pan or rolling pin, either, leaving Houston even less hope of a successful ambush on the men who ran him off a cliff that morning.

Even the ice-box is devoid of a recent block, empty except for the smell of old food and one single loaf of fossilized Wonderbread, miraculously free of mold but rendered inedible by time. Houston closes the door hard in frustration and considers tearing the faucet off the sink with his bare hands.

This strange lack of anything unnerves Houston. What *had* been here? Had anything new entered Lucas' life aside from suffering in the years since he'd come to Los Angeles? Had there only ever been rape and extortion for him here? Why hadn't he left, if there was nothing to stay for?

Maybe he was just as convinced he had nothing to go back to, Houston thinks, as he desperately searches the bathroom and comes up with nothing. It's a heartbreaking notion, and Houston wonders, helplessly, *If I'd come looking for him sooner, could I have stopped it?*

It's pointless to wonder now, and of course he looked then. For weeks, frantically; for months with wary care. Hell, even years later, he's still here looking, isn't he? Rifling through the sparse ruins of a life, for the answers he keeps hoping will make all the senselessness of it leap into clear relief. Or maybe just for the most important answer to Houston—*why did he leave me in the first place?*

There it is, in the end. It wasn't just life he walked out on, but life with *Houston*, though it's dangerous to think of it that way. Foolish to idealize what they had after the years have made clear to Houston that there is nothing idyllic left in the world they had once occupied together.

He returns to the kitchen, aimlessly opening cupboards and drawers. Houston's thoughts—and fruitless searching—are interrupted by the apartment door slamming open. He is out of time, and still unarmed—though at least in the kitchen he's off to one side and out of line of sight. The apartment door slams inward hard enough to bounce off the wall behind it and halfway closed again. Houston ducks back quickly into the kitchenette, pressing himself flat against the cabinets. From this angle, he can't see past the back of the door but he can't be seen, either.

"Come on out of there you son of a bitch," a gruff voice calls in. He has the sliding and relaxed accent Houston has come to associate with the west coast, not the city-patter that really lends a threat to that sort of language.

Houston can only see the back of the open door from his place in the kitchen. He holds his breath, waiting for an opportunity

"So help me, if I have to come in after you, I'll unload my gun into your sorry carcass and let God figure this goddamn mess out," the man yells in. Houston stays quiet, hoping his antagonist will lead with the gun through the door and give him a good opportunity to steal it.

After a moment's hesitation the goon proves himself smarter than that. He kicks the door open wide again and enters in a low stance, evading Houton's lunge for his weapon. He kicks out as Houston moves in, the heel of his shoe slamming painfully into Houston's shin and knocking him off balance and back into the kitchen. There's not much space to move in the narrow aisle between the cabinets and appliances. The man straightens out of his crouch into a menacing position as Houston looks about frantically for anything in the kitchen he's already discovered is empty.

The man doesn't give him much time to reconsider. As Houston makes a move to advance, thinking to get out of the small space, the gun comes up. Houston goes still, recognizing the confident grip on the weapon as a trained one.

"You're not the only one who knows a few tricks," the thug taunts. The gun in his hand lifts unwaveringly to draw a bead on Houston's face. He offers his hands up, palms out in unconditional surrender, hoping he has a few moments before the man shoots him at least.

"Alright, asshole, who the hell are you?" the man says, standing far enough back to keep the gun out of range of an easy grab. He has the posture and awareness of a former soldier, leaving Houston to wonder how many Mafia thugs have been trained on Uncle Sam's dime.

"I'm the guy you ran off a cliff this morning," Houston says. "You took my partner. I'm looking for him."

"Didn't learn your lesson the first time, huh?" the man shows no sign of surprise at the news. "I suppose you wouldn't, with a death wish the size of yours. Don't you know better than to mess around asking questions in Hollywood?"

"Where's my partner?" Houston demands, trying to salvage the situation. He hopes that this isn't all for nothing, but at least he would *know*.

"You're about to join him in the afterlife," his adversary assures Houston. Houston's heart sinks sharply into his gut, leaving him feeling ill. *Ex is already dead?*

He's a thinner man than Houston's ever encountered in the profession of enforcer before. He has solid shoulders anyway, and dark hair pushed back starkly from his features, held neatly in place despite his recent exertions. It lends his ocean-blue eyes a further unnatural intensity. From under the collar of his shirt, Houston can see the protruding edges of a wine-stain birthmark, patchy on one side of his neck.

"I'm damn tempted to shoot you here and let Carl sort it out," Blue-Eyes continues.

Carl, Houston figures, *must be the junkie.* He knows enough about police work to guess that Carl would be the perfect fall guy for Houston's death. No one ever trusts a junkie. He's probably on the run from the law already, and likely on the outs with the organization after today's events.

There's no reason to kill us," Houston tries. The wall at his back keeps him steady, but prevents any chance of escape. "Your boss isn't around to give orders or sign your checks anymore."

At this, Blue-Eyes' expression goes hard, angry and flashing. Houston's hit a nerve unexpectedly, dug up some kind of sewage line in the excavation of his own grave. Maybe he can use it.

"That sick bastard isn't my boss," Blue-Eyes tells Houston, glowering. "If you're very lucky you'll die before you get high enough up the food chain to worry about *my* boss. Get outside, we're going for a ride. You, me, and *my* partner."

Houston almost laughs at how cliche it sounds, a nervous response he barely keeps in check. He remembers suddenly, sitting in Edward Phillips' kitchen with a nervous college kid last year and laughing at just the idea of taking a ride. Desperate for *something* to work, Houston shoves down his nerves and blurts out, "He's a cop! The man you took with you today is a police officer."

"Not for very much longer," Blue-Eyes keeps his gun trained on Houston, but gestures at the still-open front door with his other hand to wave Houston through it.

◆ ◆ ◆

The car waiting for them with one tire up on the curb still carries the dust with it from the switchback. Houston recognizes it, black as the devil and solidly built, remembers seeing the front end with it's heavy silver fender bearing down on him. It's not that much less threatening in profile, when he's getting into it.

"Jeez, Scotty, that's really the same guy," the driver says as Houston climbs into the back seat under the constant threat of the gun trained on him. The driver is a big brick of a man, with a thick neck and shoulders that seem almost as wide as half the front bench. "I figured Carl was just off his head."

Scotty, the narrow blue-eyed man who seems to be calling the shots, climbs into the front passenger seat backwards so he can keep his gun aimed at Houston. "Yeah, well it's a damn impressive case of misplaced loyalty, I guess."

"Huh? The driver asks, turning his square head on his big neck. In profile, he has features as broad and flat as the rest of him, like a caricature of a boxer who's had his nose flattened too many times.

"He wants to know where his partner is," Scotty says. The driver laughs and starts the car.

Scotty stays turned in his seat as the car's front tire thumps down from the curb again and Houston looks hopelessly back toward the housing complex, hoping to see someone looking out the window, taking note of the strange circumstances. He sees only a wall of closed curtains, the people here either too afraid or too used to these kinds of dealings in their midst.

"I say we show him right where his partner is," Scotty says.

"You wanna go get Al?" the driver asks.

"Forget that. We got this without him. Just head out to the

coast."

As the car crunches slowly down the switchback, he tries to come up with a plan. Is his best chance to stay quiet and try to fight them when they stop, or to run when they get him out of the car, or to fight them now? None of the options give him much hope.

"You'll probably get to the party a little earlier than your buddy," Scotty says. "They had some questions... like what the hell you two assholes from Chicago are doing nosing around so far from home."

Houston holds his tongue, feeling some hope struggle up to the surface. If Ex hasn't given up any information, he might be harmed but alive. Houston won't jeopardize his chances by giving anything away. If Ex *has* already given anything up, then Houston has nothing to add. He hunches down against the back seat, resolved to wait this out in silence.

"Nothing to say now, huh?" Scotty prompts. He's still turned in his seat, gun in hand. It looks a little precarious, especially as the car grinds and bumps its way down out of Hollywood Hills on the gravel. Houston wonders if he intends to stay turned that way the whole time.

"Long ride down," the driver observes.

"Plenty of time to think. Is this what you wanted?" Scotty asks, watching Houston intently. Something in his intense gaze, mostly hidden except for the light splashing-back from the headlights against one side of his face, seems to bore into Houston. It's like he's trying to convey something, or discern something. Houston can't tell what.

"Is this what *you* wanted to happen?" Houston turns the question around, resolve forgotten. *What else is there to do?* He might still be able to *get* some information, and if he survives this, it might eventually prove useful.

"Not precisely. But we're adaptable. I'd have settled for never seeing you in this town again."

Houston wonders if that's lazy or practical, for the Mafia. After all, they have the reach and resources to deal with problems, and that might serve as the sort of deterrent the U.S. Justice System is supposed to provide.

"If you don't mind my askin'," Scotty continues, as the ride smooths out and the car pulls onto street level at last. "Why the dedication to your big dumb pal? Seems misplaced."

Sure it would, to you. Houston wonders if either of these two has any loyalty at all or if it all gets burned away in the cut-throat competition of getting to the top in the hierarchy.

"Your associate created bigger ripples than you'd think," Houston says.

"*My* associate?" Scotty trades a look with the driver.

"Williams," Houston says, watching carefully. The ghost of disgust passes back over Scotty's features, revealing it wasn't just a fluke last time.

"That guy ain't my associate."

"You sure came running quick when we started asking about him," Houston needles, attempting to draw more out. He leverages it against the idea that they won't shoot him while he's still in the car and risk the upholstery, at least.

"Yeah, well," Scotty grunts. "I got a job in asset protection. That doesn't mean I'm chummy with the assholes. Just means when some moron who doesn't know the score starts asking the wrong questions, we send a message. Figure that way they can get the idea what *not* to do in Hollywood."

Houston gets a pretty good idea of the message: *we own this town.* He wonders how much of it is true, and how much is just wishful thinking and posturing. It can't all be a show, obviously, but Houston came on a bear hunt. The question is what to do now that the bear has him.

It pans out to being a long, quiet ride in the dark while Houston reflects on what brought him here. He's found the source of the agony in Lucas' life, what drove him to alcoholism and destruction. Beyond that, he could go back deeper and deeper still. *Am I only here because I wanted to be sure it wasn't my fault?*

Houston finds the story, the whole sordid and disgusting affair now laid out in a soggy pile in some diner trash bin, tiring. He's tracked down the culprit, not quite killed him but hardly kept his vows as even a novice medical practitioner. If war taught Houston the phrase 'wouldn't piss on him to put him out,' he's only today become intimate with the sentiment.

He doesn't feel any better now that Williams is dead, because the problem goes deeper, the source comes from something bigger. Williams was only one cog in the whole steam-driven locomotive, and the great mechanized beast will pound on down the tracks without him. A cog can be replaced; it hardly matters if Houston got the specific one that's mangled him. The engine will run on to chew up others, spit them out again like the coal dust trains run on.

Houston closes his eyes, crosses his arms over his chest, and waits. Even a locomotive might derail with some leverage.

11.

The smell of the ocean reaches Houston in the depths of his thoughts before the great black expanse of the Pacific comes into view, hidden in darkness except for the slow, rolling splash and shush of waves against rocks.

They come up somewhere with a cliff's edge, not so open and public as the Santa Monica Pier, and far more deadly. *The fall will finish what the bullet doesn't,* Houston thinks as the car edges upward along the cliffside, giving him a great view of the drop. He resolves to take his chances with their guns.

"Alright, right here," Scotty instructs, and the car's tires crunch off the tarmac onto a pullout, before the driver puts it in park and shuts off the engine. Houston tenses his whole body and prepares to make a go of it, heart rate rapidly accellerating.

"Okay," Scotty instructs the driver. "You go around and get the door. I'll keep him covered."

His eyes bore into Houston's in the dim light from the car's headlamps. Warning or—*something.* He's watching Houston sharply, the barrel of his handgun trained on Houston and holding steady.

Suddenly the door next to Houston yanks open, and he lunges for the far side of the car, prying at the door handle as the driver's meaty hand grabs for him. He keeps his movement as quick and sporadic as possible, but his bet that they won't shoot into the back of their own car pays off.

"Hold still you damned—" the driver snarls, but Houston lances a kick as he works the door handle and catches him in the jaw.

He throws his whole weight against the door behind him, and then it suddenly gives way, spilling him abruptly out onto the gravel on the far side of the car.

Scotty stands over him, taking aim. "You're making this harder than it has to be."

Houston doesn't see why he should make it *easy*, as the driver moves back into view around the front of the car with a gun in *his* hand, now. Scotty starts to turn to give the man instructions, and Houston lunges sideways under the door. The driver's hand lances out and grabs the collar and shoulders of Houston's shirt, dragging him forward on his own momentum toward the rocky cliff edge. Houston is propelled along on his hands and knees and finds nothing to grab hold of to keep himself back.

The driver drops him at the precipice and presses down on the back of Houston's shoulders to keep him in place. The muzzle of his gun presses hard against the back of Houston's head, and Houston grits his teeth, eyes on the distant and jagged rocks below. He shoves up against the weight on his shoulders, helpless to budge the bigger man. He feels the driver tense to fire, and a deafening shot rings out.

Every muscle in Houston's body jerks as he jumps at the sound, ears ringing as he waits for the pain. The pressure at the back of Houston's neck goes slack slowly, and then before Houston can come up with an answer to the sum of information, the driver pitches forward over the edge of the cliff face, limp body going end-over-end once before it impacts the surf-licked rocks below with a faint thump.

Houston scrambles away from the edge of the cliff, shuffling backwards on his hands and knees and wheeling around toward Scotty. Instinctively, he raises one hand to the back of his head where the gun pressed, feeling that his skull is still whole.

"Easy," Scotty says, holding up his hands with the gun still in his right but his finger off the trigger and the muzzle pointed at the sky. "You already made this a bigger mess than I wanted."

"You—shot—" Houston gets slowly to his feet and risks a glance back over the edge to be sure of what just happened. He feels as if he can't trust his own eyes. Below, on the rocks, the waves toss the driver's body like a ragdoll, pushing and pulling it further toward the sea with each wave.

"I would have rather not," Scotty says. With his eyes locked on Houston, he slowly begins to lower his hands, sweeping his coat open to reveal the holster sitting under one arm and then tucking the gun back into it. "But it was him or you, and I hope you're not about to make me regret that."

Houston can't make heads or tails of what's happening. This man, by his own account, just shot his own partner to save Houston.

"Detective Exeter tells me you're a licensed PI in Illinois," Scotty says. "I'm inclined to believe him, but it would help me if you have your paperwork."

Houston slowly, deliberately, reaches for his wallet. "What is this?"

"This," Scotty says, "is a deliberately arranged DOJ sting operation you've just stomped all over, Mr. Mars. You could have the good grace to look a little more embarrassed by that."

Houston produces his wallet to show his license, still uncertain of the truth of the matter. It makes more sense than any other explanation he has. He hands the license over after extracting it from his wallet, and watches Scotty scrutinize the details.

"Alright, I understand that much, anyway," Scotty says. "I don't have any of my own credentials on me to show in return. I hope you can understand."

If he's operating as a planted agent, Houston supposes it's wise for the Prohi to keep the evidence somewhere that isn't on his person. He nods, numbly accepting his license back when it's returned to him.

"I'll have some questions for you, but first order of business is I gotta call this in," Scotty continues. "You're coming with me again, I'm afraid."

"Is Ex—" Houston catches himself at the edge of familiarity and corrects himself, unsure what Exeter might have told him. "Is Detective Exeter alright?"

"Sure," Scotty says. "Took some doing but I've got him down at the Van Nuys station. The worst he's been through is having to drink the station coffee all day. I was lucky not to blow my cover to do it, but I'd say I'm well and truly spent now."

He gestures back at the still-running car.

"So I guess your name isn't really Scotty?"

"No sir," Scotty says. "I'm Agent Jack White, with the DOJ prohibition office."

Somewhere in Houston's tired mind a chord strikes. The port-wine birthmark, the last name. "Your brother is looking for you."

Agent White sighs, exasperated as he settles into the driver's seat. "Yeah, Erwin never could leave anything alone."

"So, he asked you to look into this?" Jack asks, after twenty minutes of awkward silence while Houston digests the news and they make their way back into the city.

"There's—some men have been disappearing in Chicago," Houston explains. "We were looking into it when your brother—Mr. White contacted my partner—"

"Exeter?" Jack asks for clarity.

Houston recognizes the tone as officer-speak for. 'I'll verify it with the referencee', even as a stab of guilt goes through him. *I haven't exactly been good to him as a partner, or for that matter, to my actual partner.* Houston carefully sidesteps the problem in his own mind for now; it's not helpful here.

"No, my... I have a P.I. firm in Chicago," Houston says. "There's two of us. My partner there is Salvatore Costanzo. He's the one your brother called. Mr. White recognized your—birthmark, in a film."

Houston puts it as tactfully as possible, but even then he can see the color flush up under the skin on Jack's neck. "He seemed genuinely worried, and said he'd been blackmailed, too. Not anything about you being on a case, though."

"That brought you all the way to L.A.?"

"No, well... I knew a man who was a victim of one of these schemes," Houston says. "Turned out that Williams was into him personally. So I—owed it to him to come sort it out."

"Who is it? I can help you track him down if he's one of the missing out here. It wasn't my division—well, alright, I'll explain that later." Jack guides the car into a corner parking lot lit by one late night electric streetlamp. There, in the halo of the light to one corner of the intersecting streets is a police box, lit up and waiting for them. "Got radios in all their police cars now, and a special police-only band, but that only helps if you're in a police car, huh?"

Jack steps out of the driver's side and closes the door quietly behind him out of consideration for the residential area. Houston watches him pull open the box and pick up the phone inside. A sudden exhaustion overtakes Houston as he realizes it's all over. He has his answers, Exeter is safe, and all that's left is well —probably a lot of questions at the station. Then he has to explain himself to Sal and try to salvage his bank account, maybe try to get a stay on rent at the office. Maybe this thing with the Whites will pan out. He watches Jack White lean against the box in the attitude of one giving a long explanation, and Houston leans back in the passenger seat, closing his eyes against the dim street lights.

He must sleep, because he startles awake when Jack opens the driver's side door again. He sits up as Jack gets into the driver's seat.

"Do you smoke, Agent White?" Houston asks.

"Sure, some," Jack says, putting the key in the ignition. "Why?"

"Can I have a cigarette?" Houston asks, feeling the urge coil up inside him.

Jack passes over a silver cigarette case monogrammed 'S.A.' and Houston pulls a hand rolled cigarette out of it, with a tucked-in matchbook. Houston avails himself of both, and exhales out the window into the still, cool air of the night. It feels better instantly, and Houston's thoughts regain some clarity.

"His name was Lucas Harcourt," Houston answers Jack's much earlier questions. "And he's dead."

There's a long moment of silence as Jack takes his cigarette case back, something about his gaze stricken and uncertain. He pulls one of the hand-rolled cigarettes out of it, taps it twice against the metal backplate, and strikes a match after setting it between his lips.

"I knew him," Jack says. "Part of getting into this is selling it; they want some kind of insurance, I guess. Erwin told me about the blackmail letters and I made a connection. It—was even worse for the guys Williams took a special interest in."

Jack turns the car on again at last. "We gotta go in, anyway. Not a good time to be kicking up trouble. The Mafia's already mad as a bag of hornets about Williams. That your handiwork?"

"I didn't kill him," Houston says, though it's splitting hairs. "I just didn't help him when he—"

"Well if you're asking *me* about it, I say it's a fitting end," Jack says. "Nobody would ever have come forward to testify to his worst faults, and the Mafia would have bailed him back into business pretty quick. There are cops in this town that I *like*, but I don't trust them."

At the heart of things, that doesn't surprise Houston. *If you've got a rotten barrel it's only fit to hold rotten apples.* "What should I do about it?"

"Dummy up for now," Jack suggests. "The whole thing's already getting covered over because what the Mob would do to you is worse than the police, so your move was monumentally stupid. You're lucky Carl called me."

"Guess I am. Thanks for sticking your neck out."

"Yeah, well it cost me a guy I was hoping to flip at trial, but I got other tricks up my sleeve," Jack says. "Let's get you to your friend."

Houston's not sure anyone has called Exeter his friend in earnestness before.

Exeter looks tired when Jack shows Houston into the dimly lit interrogation room where Ex has been squirreled away. He's seated on the cop-side of the table for comfort or out of habit, and the table is littered with a few candy bar wrappers and paper cups, tacky with coffee remains in the bottoms.

"Where the *hell* have you been?" Exeter barks, getting up to rake his eyes over Houston like a garden full of weeds.

Houston probably looks about as well-composed as one. He is worse than rumpled, dressed in the remains of second-hand clothes and penniless. He tries to figure out how to explain succinctly. Finally, he just shakes his head. "Looking for you in all the wrong places. You couldn't call the hotel?"

"They were concerned it'd get out. There's some big bust going down. They sent an officer, but the desk clerk said you'd already come and gone."

"I was looking for you."

"Well, you found me at last. You wanna tell me about what was in that cigar box?" Exeter asks, as Houston sits down across from him.

Houston takes a second to gather his thoughts, remembering that just before they were run off the cliff, Ex was helping him get the box open. "Letters, and a few other things, but... some were from T.J. Williams."

Exeter sits back down in an attentive attitude. "Well, I'll be damned. Your guy really was tied into this porno case? I can barely believe it."

"Lucas was being manipulated," Houston tries to explain, tries to force the facts out in a logical order, but he finds he doesn't want to say all of it out loud. It's as if it's too terrible, or saying it means it's all real. He finds his voice cracking under the strain of continuing, forcing the words past the ten-pound bag of cement quick-setting in his chest. "Blackmailed. There were drugs involved."

He has to stop, with Exeter staring at him like they've never met before.

"Alright. You wanna talk about it?" Exeter says, showing a more human side than Houston's ever witnessed before.

"There was a blackmail letter from Williams. Awful stuff. A film strip with pictures of Lucas," Houston says, after a pause to get his emotions in check. "I confronted him in his office about it, but—"

"Mars," Exeter says, sitting back in his chair. "This whole thing has got you way out of whack. That shit at the apartments up in the hills..."

Ex glances at the one-way glass along one side of the room, as if checking his words on the off-chance someone was back their listening for something incriminating to charge them with. He doesn't explain further, but Houston knows what he's talking about.

"Are you done now?" Exeter asks in a tone that's not quite patronizing. "You got it out of your system?"

Houston's own father sounded much the same when he talked to Houston about the uselessness of illogical emotion. As if denial were the only strength. In this case, however noxious the reminder of his father is, however little he'd like to think of his family in this situation, he's been overboard beyond excuse in his actions.

"I know," Houston admits. "You got a cigarette?"

Exeter comes up with one. Houston accepts it, and the matchbook, then passes the matches back when he's lit. It's enough of a pause that Houston can start getting his thoughts in order. It's a lot to deal with.

"I'm done," Houston says. He finds that in his heart, he's ready to go home. Back to Chicago and the cold, except it's a mess there, too. He tore out his roots to get this far. "I got to the bottom of it, but it's a systemic infection, like sepsis."

Exeter gives him a sympathetic glance. "It wasn't worth it?"

"I don't know if anything you do for someone who's already dead is worth it."

"It is if it's what it takes for you to let things rest."

Houston considers that, and then does his best to accept it.

"I gotta come clean about something," Ex starts, unexpectedly. Now it's his turn to delay with a cigarette and the process of lighting it.

"You're not here because Sal sent you," Houston summarizes.

"I'm not *only* here because your partner said he was worried about your behavior," Exeter admits. "Dan O'Halloran sent me."

"*O'Halloran?*" Houston demands, wanting to get to the bottom of this. "What's he got you do—"

Just then the door swings open, admitting the harsh electric yellow light from the hallway. Jack pokes his head in. He's changed out of the slouchy clothes he'd been wearing and dressed his hair back from his face in a more professional style. Houston catches Exeter *looking*, and realizes he's not been exactly subtle in checking the guy out either.

"Hate to step in and interrupt," Jack says with the air of one vexedly amused by something. "But there's a call for you. Rather, about you."

"What?" Houston asks.

"There's two men from Chicago at the downtown L.A. precinct asking some very difficult questions," Jack says. "They're trying to report you missing. It's putting me in a tough place."

Sal, Houston realizes, though he can't figure who he's brought with him. *What a mess.* "Can I talk to them?"

Jack beckons Houston along to a bank of phones in a receiver room that also includes radio equipment for the L.A. police's new exclusive radio station. He picks a phone receiver up off the table where it's been holding the line open.

Houston holds it up to his ear. "Sal, did you really come all the way to California?"

"*Houston,*" Sal's voice sounds both relieved and like he might really be angry. "I took a flight right after your call. I've been all over this damn city. Did you find Exeter?"

"Turns out I never really lost him," Houston says, instinctively glancing back up the hall over Jack's shoulder like Exeter might be sneaking out the back even now. "Yeah, I found him, he's safe. I am, too."

"That was my next question. Where are you?"

Houston makes eye-contact with Jack, who is obviously listening in to Houston's end of the conversation but attempting to be unobtrusive about it. He covers the receiver mic with his cupped palm. "It's my partner. Can I tell him where we are?"

"Will he kick up more of a ruckus if you don't? You're *supposed* to be missing, remember," Jack says. "At least as far as the Mafia's concerned."

"Houston?" Sal's voice against his ear.

"He should know," Houston says.

"Alright, tell him. But let him know to keep it close to his chest."

Houston remembers Jack's earlier words about cops he likes versus cops he trusts.

"Houston," Sal repeats.

"Hang on," Houston says, then has to repeat himself after pulling his hand away from the phone. "Sal, I'll explain when you get here, but try not to celebrate too publically and you should walk away without answering any questions from cops."

"Alright," Sal sounds guarded but attentive. "This better be *some* story."

"Come down to the Van Nuys police station and I'll tell you what I can."

"Got it," Sal says. "But, uh, you should know, I got Dan O'Halloran with me."

"*Hell,*" Houston swears, and a spike of pure adrenaline shocks his exhausted system, guilty and hot like a knife in his side. He fights off a wave of juvenile panic. "What for?"

"Exeter, apparently."

"I'd bet that's not the *only* reason he came along."

"Listen," Sal lowers his voice. "This is a big, complicated thing.

Let's sort it out when we get there, okay?"

Houston heart gives a slow, heavy thud in his chest. It's coming —it's been coming since the beginning. All he can do is answer. "Okay."

"I gotta go get some things together," Jack says, returning Houston to the room with Exeter. "You guys are free to go if you need to, but don't leave town. It would help me and you out if you lay low."

"How long will you be?" Houston asks.

"Round ups, shake ups, and arrests," Jack explains. Even his bright, attentive blue eyes are starting to show some signs of being tired. "Could take a while, but I still have some questions for you folks. Could have saved me a lot of trouble if you'd just made your move a few days later."

"Sorry," Houston expresses the platitude he doesn't really feel. "What about Sal? He's on the way here."

"Stay until he gets here, then leave your hotel address on the desk. Gimme twenty-four hours to wrap this up. I'm extending a courtesy I wouldn't except you're obviously beat, and one of you is a cop."

There's not a lot of tough-guy in the tone, but warning enough that Houston takes it seriously. "We'll stay. A full day of sleep sounds about like what I need."

Jack yawns broadly in answer, and heads out to do his job. Houston slumps down in the chair opposite Exeter again and feels exhaustion settle around his shoulders like a cloak.

"Did you say Costanzo is coming?" Exeter asks. "That's a long trip."

"He's already in the city," Houston explains. "I called him... yesterday afternoon I guess it was. He took a flight."

Exeter whistles. "That's some dedication."

"Yeah." Houston feels another stab of guilt for his indiscretion with the reporter. *Did O'Halloran tell him about it?* "Well, we may be in for rougher times, yet. Anyway, he says O'Halloran is with him."

"Shit. This gets bigger and bigger."

"You were starting to tell me why you really came along, Ex?"

"I *really* came along 'cause you were acting off your damn rocker. I was in the train station to buy a ticket anyway. Imagine my damn surprise when you bought the same one."

"Ex, you didn't bring a suitcase."

Exeter looks away, seeming embarassed. "I was gonna stop in at Ma's in San Francisco, but not with you around."

Houston sighs. "And O'Halloran sent you here?"

"O'Halloran put me on a missing persons case related to some porno stars," Exeter says. "He said it could be traced back to this Williams guy. I didn't know it was the same case you were onto until Jack grabbed me—and scared the *shit* out of me, by the way."

Houston puts it together slowly. "*That's* why you were at O'Halloran's the other day."

Exeter lifts one of his meaty paws to rub the back of his neck in a surprisingly sheepish gesture. "Yeah, we have an—he brings me busts, and when I make 'em, he breaks the news. I always let him have the first scoop. This was a big one, though I guess it's all shot to hell now."

Houston measures Exeter up, reclaiming the cigarette he'd left to go out earlier and relighting. He finds it doesn't even seem that strange for a cop and a reporter to play a little scratch-my-back game in the current desperate world. *So that's what keeps*

O'Halloran on the payroll.

"Imagine my surprise to see you walking out of there, then catch O'Halloran half-naked and guilty as a cat in the cupboard," Exeter continues. "I know *he* has a rap like that, but I'd have figured you were too smart to fall for it."

"Gee, thanks, Ex."

Exeter glances at the one-way glass again, belatedly as if realizing he's just incriminated them both. "Anyway, I haven't exactly had the luxury time to track down those poor missing dopes, so it's a bust for O'Halloran, anyway, and I'm about out of vacation time."

"You shouldn't have to worry about Williams anymore."

"Oh yeah?"

"He's dead." The statement enters the atmosphere of the room like a cold breeze.

The words may not surprise Exeter, but he goes quiet for a while afterward.

They part ways as they leave the Van Nuys station, Sal taking possession of Houston and Exeter leaving with O'Halloran. Houston makes an urgent request to stop to pick up the cigar box, but they ride in silence otherwise.

By the time they make it back to the motel Sal's taken a room at, Houston is dozing against the rear window of the cab. Sal's kept his response to the situation contained for now by some miracle of composure that Houston does his best to follow along with. It means he's contained his initial relief at seeing Sal, feeling it wash against him like a warm summer tide.

He still feels comforted by Sal's presence. As they climb the short flight of stairs up to the second floor of the motel, a sink-ing feeling weighs on Houston like an anchor. He has a lot of explaining to do.

"We're in eight," Sal directs, brusquely. He gestures toward a door on their left, painted in a thick coat of rust-red paint with a brass number eight affixed to the door above a pair of decorative wooden palm trees crossed in a crude x-shape.

From his pocket, he produces a key with a shaped plastic fob —also a palm tree. The lock opens stubbornly, and inside the room is appointed in a standard no-frills style. Two beds, a nightstand, a cube of a bathroom in the back and a table with an ashtray on it, attended by a single chair. Morning light is coming through the gauzy curtain, as dawn finishes breaking.

Houston slumps onto one of the beds, as Sal crosses the space and steps into the bathroom. Houton hears the water run, and then Sal appears with a glass of water in his hand and hesitates in the door of the bathroom, looking at Houston.

"Well?" Sal asks.

"Well, I—found T.J. Williams," Houston says. "He was every bit the bastard you'd expect."

"Any leads on our missing persons?" Sal asks. "Or were you too focused on whatever brought you here?"

Houston's too tired to do anything but let the barb stand. He's got some good news, but he can't take any credit for it, being that it's hardly due to his detective work.

"Did Mr. White ever tell you what his brother does for a living?" Houston asks.

"No, just that he was missing. After that it was more about what happened than who it happened to."

"So, his brother's a Prohibition Agent, and I ran into him—and I guess Ex and I blew his cover."

"No shit?" Sal seems genuinely surprised. "Hell. That's on me. I'll ask more direct questions next time."

"Anyway, he's safe, and it's a long story. I came looking to see if I could figure out what contributed to Lucas' death. And it all seemed to point in the same direction."

"So you left without me."

Houston fights off his initial defensive response and lets the accusation stand. There's no use denying the bald truth of it. "I did. You had a case of your own and you'd told me to leave it. I couldn't."

"Clearly," Sal says. His expression in the dim sunrise light is flinty but not without sympathy. He shifts in the doorway. "You could have come to me."

"I—" Houston hits the roots of the matter, then. He feels too tired to keep running from it. "I felt guilty. I didn't know how to face you, but I could face this. I had to."

Sal's eyebrows draw in, and a concerned expression creeps onto his features "I don't know what to make of that statement, Hobbes. What were you feeling guilty about?"

Houston isn't sure how to approach this, what angle to come at it from, if there's a good one at all. There's the heavy weight of Sal's gaze sitting expectantly on Houston's shoulders. He lifts a hand and rubs his face. It feels gritty.

"I cheated on you," Houston says, trying it on for size. It doesn't feel quite right, but it drops out of Houton like the plug in the bottom of a boat. "I stepped out."

"Houston," Sal cuts in, stepping forward. "It's not like we're married. It's not even like we're *dating*."

The words cut, and Houston recoils, cold at the small of his back. There's something on Sal's expression, too. A reservation that Houston wonders about. They've hurt each other, and Houston feels it like a lead weight.

"Sal, come on, it's more than a casual fling."

"More than that, less than the rest. You and I know it can't really be anything else."

Houston wishes he could argue otherwise, but with things the way they are, and the world in general hostile, it's not easy. They both knew it from the start, and that they'd face it someday.

"Sal, I'm sorry," Houston says, heartfelt. "I shouldn't have ever done it and I won't ask you to forgive me."

"I'll take it into consideration," Sal sighs. "But... I get it. You're like an addict with this stuff about Lucas. Can you let it go, now? Have you chased it far enough?"

Subconsciously, Sal's hand drifts to the small of his back, rubbing absently at the ache there. Houston supposes his behavior has been almost as off-kilter as a junkie's. He's been chasing an itch, finding it difficult to scratch, needing more and more.

"Yeah, I guess I got my fix," Houston says. "I found a bunch of letters. Some from Williams. It was terrible, Sal."

"Did you have any expectation that it would be otherwise? You dug into it *because* you knew it was going to be bad."

"I had the instinct it would be, but I guess I wasn't prepared for how it would actually be."

"It's not like you to just jump into things."

"I couldn't stop thinking about it. I have the answers now, and I'm sure I don't want to think about it anymore."

"For now," Sal says. "What about the next time someone dangles something about his past in front of you?"

Houston thinks about it as a hypothetical. "I don't know. For now, I'm too tired to think about it."

"You look like hell. And those clothes don't look much better. I brought a change for you, but you should wash up and sleep first."

"I agree." Houston drags himself up from the edge of the bed, and brushes by Sal on the way to the bathroom. He stops, and looks up from the floor to meet Sal's gaze. "Thanks, Sal. I'm a louse, but I appreciate that you came through for me."

"You bet I did." Sal's expression softens a little. "Your cat misses you."

"Chop Suey." Houston hopes no real danger came to the cat. "Thanks for that, too. How much are you out after all this?"

Sal turns the question around again like a knife. "How much are *you* out?"

"We... may not make rent on the office," Houston admits. "I hope your case is paying."

"Hmm," is all Sal says. He closes the bathroom door behind Houston and leaves him with the company of his own thoughts.

12.

Jack calls on them at the motel the next evening, tapping softly on the door.

"We better all eat so it's amicable," Jack explains, looking surprisingly rested for a man who was out all night. "Nothing makes a man mean like being hungry, and Halward tells me you haven't exactly made a leisurely trip of it."

It takes Houston a minute to figure out that Jack means Exeter. He's pretty sure the last meal he ate was half a hotel breakfast two days ago. The thought makes him hungry. "I suppose not. The sleep's been lousy too, 'til now."

Jack laughs. "All those Hollywood lights will go to your head, that's for sure."

Exeter and Dan O'Halloran are waiting downstairs in the open courtyard. O'Halloran trails behind with his stenographer's pad at the ready like he might need it to ward off a lion at any second.

"Hey, Mars, you look better than the last time I saw you," O'Halloran greets.

The last thing Houston wants to think about is the last time he and O'Halloran saw each other, and it takes him a minute to realize the reporter means 'this morning.' Houston answers with a noncommittal sound, and they all pile into Jack's car.

It's a quiet ride, and the silence is frosty and uncomfortable with Houston trapped in the back seat between Sal and O'Halloran. The city is alive around them with the evening crowd, and Jack doesn't take them too far. After a brief discussion with

Jack they decide on a diner. It's later in the evening, but like Chicago there are enough graveyard workers to support an overnight establishment on every other corner.

The diner is sedately decorated for the area, and the cooking food fills the inside with a warm, welcoming scent—bacon and eggs and hot batter that transports Houston back to the kitchen of his childhood. He can remember the cool, polished wood tabletop under his palms, and nudging his older brother under the table with his shoe as his mother cooked the family breakfast.

They take a table in the corner, and the waitress brings them a whole pot of coffee and leaves them to fill their own cups.

"How'd your bust go down?" O'Halloran asks first, an eager expression on his sharp features.

"Lots of unhappy folks today," Jack says. "We pulled mostly from up the food chain so it'll take everyone left a couple days to sort out how mad they are about it."

"Can I pry any names out of ya?" O'Halloran presses shamelessly.

"You can shut up and listen and see what you can put together," Jack says, giving O'Halloran a barely restrained dirty look. "If you're gonna be a twerp you can go sit somewhere else until I have a question for you."

O'Halloran's foxy features compose themselves into the attitude of a listening school child, green eyes sharp. The waitress approaches their group and takes their orders. Houston tries ordering lightly, until Sal elbows him in the side and overrides him with an order for a full breakfast.

"So, I should ask you about the situation with Williams." Jack pours a hefty measure of sugar into his coffee, stirring so vigorously the spoon clanks against the sides of the mug. "What's your side of that?"

Houston goes quiet for a moment to sort his thoughts out carefully. "I found some letters in Lucas' old apartment. They were from Williams, addressed to Lucas."

"That the bundle you sent me?" Sal asks, reminding Houston that he sent some along before confronting Williams. Some of the most incriminating ones, and the film strip.

"Yes!" Houston gushes, relieved. "Did you get it?"

"How the hell would I have gotten it? It's a safe bet it'll be waiting for us when we get back."

Jack watches the conversation progress like he's a tennis spectator, eyes alert. "May I inquire as to what the details of these letters were?"

"Blackmail, mostly. Some description of what kinds of shit Williams got up to with the fellas he was so keen on hiring," Houston says. "I was livid, reading it all. He was so sure Lucas would be too ashamed to do anything about how vile he was."

"Well," Jack says. "I take your point, and I don't wanna spoil anyone's breakfast. You say you've still got the letters?"

"Some of them," Houston pushes his coffee cup around in a circle on the table. "I took a few with me to confront him. Those got burned up along with my shirt."

"Explains the state I found you in."

Houston becomes aware of O'Halloran's scribbling pen. He tries to disregard it but an overdue guilt about the events overtakes him. He's concerned that in putting the truth about Williams out, he's going to show off a side of his near-mania about the case that he's only just coming to terms with. *Still, it's going to be out there. If not in my own words, then in O'Halloran's.*

"I went in to confront him. I wasn't too polite about it, I guess. He didn't really deserve politeness, either. He denied everything, until I pulled out some of the letters, and then there was a scuffle over them. I dropped my cigarette and his carpet went up a little. While we were beating each other up, he tipped over his cart full of booze. Spilled all over the carpet. He stepped in it."

O'Halloran looks up at Houston with thirsty eyes. "Damned waste, with Prohibition on."

Jack's gaze slowly peels itself off Houston to land with obvious reproval on O'Halloran, who actually shifts as if it hits him physically, offering a shrug in response to the silent accusation.

"Uh, of valuable evidence," O'Halloran appends, "for court."

"So you admit you fought him," Jack says. "But you didn't kill him?"

"We fought. The fire killed him," Houston says. Sal is looking at him very seriously, and Exeter seems to be doing some kind of mental math. "I just didn't render any aid."

It's the sort of thing he hasn't said since the end of the war, the sort of justification for inhumanity based on the status of 'enemy' or 'ally.' Houston only rarely refused aid to even Axis soldiers. This outstrips that to an unprecedented degree for Houston.

Jack reaches for the coffee pot and refills his cup, considering the information without saying anything yet. In the tense pause, the waitress senses an opportunity to quickly set down their plates of food, and exchange the mostly empty coffee pot for a second. O'Halloran arranges his plate to one side so he can keep his dominant hand on the steno pad, ready to write.

"That's manslaughter," Exeter says when she's gone, apparently done with his mental addition.

"I wasn't touching him," Houston says. "But I wouldn't have stuck myself back into a burning room for that ass, and you wouldn't have done it, either."

"Well," Jack gently interposes. "We found enough evidence of blackmail and other sins in his files that the firemen working the scene were shocked. Pictures, film. He kept it all in a filing cabinet right there in his office. Pretty lurid stuff."

"Shit," Houston says, and he feels his appetite wavering again.

"I've got Erwin forwarding his letters to me," Jack says. "He was pissed when I called, but I couldn't exactly have cut him into the loop. My bet's it'll match a typewriter somewhere in Williams' possession—at home, maybe."

"At the very least, you might be able to match origin points by the postage, if you can't get the rest out of his records," Houston says. "He was the sort who probably got off on good book-keeping and holding on to records of his past conquests."

"Notches on the bedpost," O'Halloran puts in around a mouthful of toast, still writing furiously.

You would know, Houston thinks uncharitably. "But it's not as if you can charge the man."

"The man himself, no. The men behind the operation who empowered and protected him, that we can make a try at," Jack says. "Even if that feels a little like running at windmills, most of the time."

"Sure. You don't get an office on Sunset Boulevard as a kidnapper and blackmailer all on your own," O'Halloran puts in.

"No, these days you need bankroll, and there's only one organization making enough money with few enough scruples."

"What about the other missing men?" Exeter asks. "From Chicago?"

"They've got 'em holed up somewhere," Jack says. "Probably close to a production studio so they can keep cranking out the films until they wear this batch out. Then they'll find the folks they think might have other uses, pull them out with the threat of public disgrace and humiliation over their heads and make use of 'em."

There's a distant look on Jack's face. For a moment, all four of the men in the booth fall silent while that sinks in. Houston guiltily picks up his fork and has at his eggs, trying to appease his empty belly while there's a lull. Jack takes a long sip of coffee and his gaze slides to Exeter and O'Halloran. Houston realizes they don't know about Jack's own experience with such productions, so he resolves to talk around it.

"I've got a few hunches," Jack says, after lengthening his pause with a bite of breakfast. "We're looking into Mafia owned and front properties in the area. We'll find them."

"You think that's gonna be fast enough?" Exeter asks. "If they figure out what you're looking for, they may decide it's better to kill the whole group and dispose of the evidence."

Jack nods, acknowledging that it's a real possibility. "I'm hoping we shook 'em up enough that they don't know what's going on with Williams' establishment. We're trying to keep it out of the news that it was anything other than just a fire."

He stops to look at O'Halloran pointedly.

"Don't look at me, pal," O'Halloran holds up his ink-stained hands and grins almost charmingly at Jack. "I'm with the *Tribune*. It'll be breaking news there, but I've got to get back to my beat, first."

"Don't phone ahead," Jack warns, this time full of the dry iron of military command. "If I found out you broke this before I get those men out of there, I'll come after you."

"You think I'd mess with federal justice?" O'Halloran grimaces, putting on a pained look like a dog eating something he doesn't like. "You wound me."

"I'll do worse than that," Jack lets the threat dangle unfinished. Houston suspects it's enough.

"Anyway," Jack continues after a sip of refilled and re-sweetened coffee. "I'm not gonna try and make a manslaughter case stick when the victim was barely a man to begin with, but the incident will go on your record, Houston."

O'Halloran is back to his furious scribbling and Exeter is looking at Houston with an expression that could freeze the blood in his veins even in the sunny California atmosphere.

"I think you lot should leave town," Jack says. "I'll take your signed statements and come collect that material evidence, but we'll be sorting the rest out for trial for a while, and a lot of these guys got real good laywers. I don't promise they won't make bail and be out walking around, getting curious why we got so lucky with the Williams office."

"What about you?" Exeter asks. "You were at the forefront of this thing. Hell, you were right in the middle of it. They all know what you look like, and none of these guys exactly take kindly to double-crossing. If they give these guys bail...."

"Might get real ugly," Jack agrees. "But I'm a federal agent with the DOJ. Puts me at a level removed from law enforcement officers or self-employed. I'll make out. And I keep real good paperwork, just in case."

Houston wishes that made him feel more confident. Instead, he goes quiet again, pushing his breakfast around on his plate. He has most of the pieces now, or enough that the picture lines up with the jumble dumped in his lap last December. He should feel satisfied, but instead he feels hollowed out and lost, uncertain of his own future in this new landscape he's carved for himself.

In a way, the rudderless uncertainty feels like when he'd stepped back off the boat and onto American soil, the surety that he should be feeling something but that there's no appropriate emotion and nothing to guide his steps.

"I won't do it," Houston says, as Sal repacks his suitcase.

"Be reasonable," Sal strains to click his overstuffed and messily packed suitcase closed. "You've been gone like a week already, and if we fly back we might make it back in time to keep the landlord from putting all our office furniture out on the street."

"Or we could crash and die, and then nobody would feed my cat."

Sal gives Houston a look. "I only barely managed to talk Miss Wentz into feeding Chop Suey for the time it took me to get out here and drag you back."

"Well," Houston says, stubbornly. "If you wanna fly back, I'll meet you there."

Sal keeps looking at him, shaking his head.

"Train's cheaper fare anyway," Houston points out.

"Yep," Sal hoists his suitcase over his shoulder and concedes the argument, seeming too tired to insist on having it his way. "But if we're going by train, we're going now."

Houston doesn't disagree. He's ready to put the whole ordeal behind him. He does up the buttons on the shirt Sal brought him from home and follows Sal out of the motel room. He taps his knuckles on the wooden palm trees for good luck as they leave.

"You better be reasonable about everything else on the way back," Sal warns, after turning in their key.

"You know about how reasonable I am by now." Houston follows him toward the bus stop.

"And here I am, anyway."

Later, once they're settled into a train car, Houston feels the weight of exhaustion mantling around his shoulders again. He settles into the rear-facing seat and leans his cheek against the window, watching L.A. recede away. As they leave, the hills and the HOLLYWOODLAND sign are invisible.

"So you really spent all our money on this crusade?" Sal asks, settling down across from Houston with a paper cup of coffee from the dining car.

Too late, Houston realizes the error of his decision. They'd be alone in a train car for days, even accounting for time to sleep. Plenty of time to talk out all the problems Houston's been avoiding.

"Not all of it," Houston says, doing a little mental math. "I'm sure there's still something in the company savings account, but not enough to cover the rent on our office this month. You think what we're expecting from Erwin will help?"

Sal sits back, mouth closed and arms crossed over his chest. The train gives a lurch, and then stops, waiting for another one to cross its path before easing into motion again. "In a way."

Houston tries not to mirror the closed-off posture. Instead, he does his best to bridge the gap. "I'm sorry about this whole thing. Maybe we can get the deposit back and find a cheaper place in another part of town."

Sal arches his eyebrows. Houston doesn't think he was expecting an apology. Houston gets his thoughts together a little more on the subject, with a guilty glance toward the hall before forging on. "I've been thoughtless—careless—about your feelings."

"Hell," Sal says, cutting Houston off sharply. "Don't give me some talk like we're married and you violated a sacred vow. We're still partners, aren't we?"

Houston supposes they are. "For whatever that means, given that we might not have an office."

"It means we're partners," Sal insists, firmly. "I'm not giving you a free pass to keep waddling around with your head up your ass, mind. But, you carried me when I was heavy and that's one thing we both learned in the war."

Houston meets Sal's eyes and sees he means it. So, they have what they have, for what it's worth. Like the whole suffering country does, for now. Houston feels himself smiling on impulse, and the slow thaw at the center of his soul is like winter might be ending at last.

"Thanks, Sal."

"I don't wanna hear about it anymore," Sal sighs. "If you do it again, I don't wanna hear about it then, either. The world we live in is kinda impermanent."

Houston accepts the admonishment and resolves to be better. To get out of the past. Sal and Lucas aren't entirely dissimilar, but Sal is tempered and grounded by his wartime experiences. Since he's left off opium, he's had his feet on the ground. He still has moments of capricious uncollectedness, but he's steady at his core and that's a fundamental difference.

"I won't do it again."

"Good. For the record, I prefer you don't."

Houston accepts the terms, then his thoughts touch back to earlier in the conversation. "What'd you mean earlier? About how Erwin will help us, in a way?"

"Oh," Sal actually chuckles. "Well I took out a work agreement in trade. Didn't know if we'd make good on it, but we've got an office space free of charge, so long as you don't mind the environs."

"The—?" Houston takes a moment for it to sink in. They have very little choice, except for some sort of miracle. Still, better to know the details. "What environs?"

"Mr. White is one of the partners that owns the Sappho," Sal explains. "One of the upstairs rooms has been converted to an office, but these days all the administration is conducted offsite. It's ours if we want it. Hell of a lot better than asking my *family* for another loan."

Houston sinks back in his seat, more surprised by this revelation than many others in the past week. His thoughts churn on the subject. It will be tough to get good-paying clientele at the Sappho, and set them up as practically advertising their sexualities.

There are still frequent raids on the Sappho, though if Houston keeps his business license up to date, they can avoid some of the hassle. It will undoubtedly make some things more complicated. *Then again,* Houston thinks, *the price is right, and it's not like we don't already have the reputation. It's where the last two cases came from.*

It's never really been about the big money, anyway, and in the current economy, there's little opportunity to change that. He looks up from his thoughts to find Sal waiting expectantly for an answer.

"You're a genius," Houston says, genuinely grateful. "But we're going to have to get our desks down all those stairs."

Sal wrinkles his nose and digs in his suit pocket for his cigarettes. "I was hoping we'd just get new desks delivered."

EPILOGUE.

"**S**o I hit that exclusive on the Winsome case, and you know what my rat-fink boss does?" O'Halloran grunts as he makes his way downstairs with the burden of a heavy box containing tax files and administrative documents. Nothing interesting, after he was caught sticking his nose into the case files with daring curiosity.

"What'd he do?" Sal asks, leaning on the banister at the bottom of the stairs as Houston and O'Halloran make their way down with the last of their belongings from upstairs. He has one hand tucked up under the hem of his suit-coat against the small of his back, telling a clear story of where the pain is.

Accepting the straight man line, O'Halloran passes Houston at the bottom of the stairs. "He dumped me back on page five with it. Says it's 'old news.' As if that fratricide Winsome guy isn't on trial this week. The Tribune's all changed gear onto the Mafia."

"Well, you got in on there too, right?" Houston asks. "You were getting the jump on it in California. That's what you had Ex out there for?"

"Yeah, and that was good a week ago," O'Halloran grunts, dropping the box into Houston's arms so he can carry it to the car. Houston's shoulder gives a warning twinge. "This is the news business. They want the Chicago half now."

"Hey, speaking of Ex, why isn't that big gorilla helping us out with the heavy lifting?" Sal says, as Houston tries to find a place to lodge the box of taxes in Sal's already overloaded Ford.

"I don't think he likes us that much," Houston says.

"Well, for that big oaf, he likes to keep up appearances. Consorting with the likes of you and me, he could lose his job," O'Halloran says. "He's already on thin ice after last year, and he only barely made it back while he still had vacation time."

Houston jams the crate into the passenger seat, and slides his hands into his pockets, nodding. He knows that Exeter has been busy working the Chicago half of the case since his return.

"Anyway, your boy Jack promised he'd lynch me if he read this in the paper before he found those guys—and lynch me *twice* if he saw my byline on it," O'Halloran says. "But they found those missing guys finally and sprung 'em. They been through hell, and probably they're facing another one giving testimony, but they're alive."

Houston feels a faint triumph at that, followed by a sadness it hadn't come soon enough for Lucas. For them, they might get out and get past it. Houston can feel the key secreted in one pocket. He put it there when he was cleaning out his desk drawers earlier, and now rubs it between his fingers like a talisman.

"That's one positive," Houston says, and O'Halloran's fox-sharp eyes hone in on him, his tongue wetting his lower lip like he's looking at a delicious prey animal. "Too bad it wasn't soon enough for your old flame, eh?"

"Hey, shut it off for a minute, will you?" Sal steps in, and O'Halloran holds his hands up in surrender, backing up a step. "This ain't your next break."

"Nah. Just—wondering if that lead would turn up any new ones. This old hound dog loves a chase, huh?" O'Halloran jerks a thumb at Houston indicatively. "So if anybody's gonna dig up any old bones on this, it's Detective Mars, here."

They handed the rest of the cigar box contents over to Jack White as evidence a week ago. Something made Houston keep the little locker key Lucas had left in it. He put it in his desk drawer, then found it again today as he cleaned out his desk. One last thread to unravel. Houston closes his hand on the key in his pocket and shakes his head at O'Halloran.

"Well, we got everything?" Sal asks, leaning against his overloaded car, one hand pressed to the small of his back again.

"Yep," Houston says. "That's it. Thanks for the help, O'Halloran."

"You can call me Dan," O'Halloran says, stretching his arms over his head. "You can call me next time you got a big scoop, too."

"What about the next time we need to move?" Sal asks.

"No, then you can forget my number," O'Halloran chuckles, and tips his hat to them, taking his exit before he can be asked to help unload everything again at their destination.

"I'd rather not call him at all," Houston grumbles.

Sal trades a knowing look with Houston. "As my Ma always says, I got a date with the Laudanum bottle."

"Sal." Houston doesn't find the joke funny.

"Alright, well, I want some nyalgesic anyway. And a burger. I'm starved."

"Gimme just a minute," Houston says, turning back toward the building. Sal trails after, as if worried. Inside, Houston leans into Miss Wentz's little switchboard closet.

"Here's the key, Miss Wentz," Houston says, offering the office key to her, and leaving the one from his desk in his pocket.

"Gee, Huey, Mr. Costanzo," Miss Wentz looks them both over with genuine remorse on her features. "I'll be sad you guys aren't around anymore, you know? The lawyers are going out this month, too."

"We'll miss you too, Miss Wentz."

"Make sure you come back with your forwarding number when you're all set up, okay? So I can pass it along when someone asks.

Give Chop Suey a pat for me, huh? He's a sweetheart and he's had a rough time."

Houston notices her optimism and finds he really will miss her, even if he won't miss the nicknames, or the narrow stairway up or the dismal view from his office window. He's betting he'll miss the short commute, though. "Of course. And if you ever need any help...."

Houston isn't sure they have much to offer her, but she smiles gratefully at him and nods. She puts her graceful hand out firmly to shake his, then Sal's hand in turn. Her grip is firm and decisive, and they all wish each other good luck and mean it.

At the curb, Houston eyes Sal's overloaded Ford with one hand on the key remaining in his pocket. He decides. "I'll meet you there."

"Yeah, honestly, the bus'll probably be less crowded," Sal agrees. "See you south of the Loop. Soon as possible, huh? I'm dying to eat."

Houston watches the tottering jalopy roll away and boards the next bus for Central Station.

Chicago's Central Station is all wide open architecture, columns and stately open walkways that bustle with people at all hours. Houston checks the locker number stamped on the key against the row of lockers along the side wall, and then locates the right one.

There's nothing special about it, the front painted in a thick, rust colored coat of paint like all the others. It has a small metal plate affixed to it with a pair of screws, printed with the same number as the key in his hand.

Houston puts the key in the lock and wonders what it was Lucas left behind for himself, or if he came back to Chicago for it, only to find he'd left the key, or in spite of not having it. The lock opens, trapping the key in the mechanism once he's turned it, and he swings the door out.

The locker is empty, a bare metal cube in front of him. Houston puts his hand inside and feels the walls, top and floor of the space. Nothing. The metal is cool to the touch. Houston steps back and checks the number on the key and the door it's stuck in again. It's the right locker.

Houston helplessly stares into the empty space, and tries to figure out the next step. A disheveled man several lockers down catches Houston's attention.

"They empty 'em every three months or so," he advises in a sympathetic tone. "You have to come in and keep moving lockers, man. If it hasn't been too long they might still have the stuff, if you ask at the desk."

Houston doesn't know how long it's been, but he thanks the man anyway. The empty locker resounds in Houston harder than he expects it to, but it makes Houston think, too. He looks across the station at the service desk.

He leaves the key and the empty locker behind, and exits the station into the cooling evening, letting the page turn on a very long chapter in his life.

The End.

ABOUT THE AUTHOR

B. A. Black

B.A. Black is an Arizona based author who devides time between several enthusiasms, though the first will always be writing. Five cats share the house and each lends a little helping hand with inspiration for Chop Suey as well as distracting from work on the next Houston Mars novel.

BOOKS IN THIS SERIES

Houston Mars

Set in the 1930's and with a distinctively noir style, the Houston Mars mysteries explore the adventures of Houston Mars and his partner Salvatore Costanzo as they investigate the cases most cops don't care enough to solve.

Cold Was The Ground

The first of the Houston Mars mysteries. Houston and his partner Salvatore investigate the sudden disappearance of a Steel Magnate's son.

A HUMBLE REQUEST

I f you enjoyed this work, please leave a favorable review on the site you purchased it from. Independent and Self Published authors rely on you, the reader, for success instead of major marketing campaigns. The author of this book and authors of other self published books thank you in advance!

Made in the USA
Middletown, DE
06 June 2021

40577653R00116